Acclaim for Jon S. Lewis

"Non-stop, action-packed thrills and ... put down ... [a] cliffhanger that left n ...

—SciFiChick.com, regarding *Alienation*

"Mechanical spiders, jet packs, Nazi/alien alliances, and characters with names like Borog and Zandarr will render certain readers putty in Lewis' capable hands."

—*Booklist* review of *Invasion*

"[A] fast-paced and well-defined world will keep readers glued to the pages."

—*School Library Journal* review of *Invasion*

"Lewis is a veteran of the comic-book industry, and his plot is a domestic read-alike of Alex Rider."

—*Kirkus Reviews*, regarding *Invasion*

"A fun read."

—*Publishers Weekly* review of *Invasion*

"... Crackling plot twists, cliffhanger chapter endings, cyber attacks, alien invaders, and an undercurrent of teen romance."

—*BookViews* by Alan Caruba, regarding *Invasion*

DOMINATION

The C.H.A.O.S. Trilogy

3

ALSO BY JON S. LEWIS

Invasion
Alienation

DOMINATION

The C.H.A.O.S. Trilogy

3

JON S. LEWIS

THOMAS NELSON
Since 1798

NASHVILLE   DALLAS   MEXICO CITY   RIO DE JANEIRO

Published in Nashville, Tennessee, by Thomas Nelson. Thomas Nelson is a registered trademark of Thomas Nelson, Inc.

Thomas Nelson, Inc., books may be purchased in bulk for educational, business, fund-raising, or sales promotional use. For information, please e-mail SpecialMarkets@ThomasNelson.com.

Author is represented by the literary agency of Alive Communications, Inc., 7680 Goddard Street, Suite 200, Colorado Springs, CO 80920, www.alivecommunications.com

Library of Congress Cataloging-in-Publication Data

Lewis, J. S. (Jon S.)
    Domination : a C.H.A.O.S. novel / Jon S. Lewis.
        pages cm. — (A C.H.A.O.S. novel ; 3)
    Summary: Sixteen-year-old Colt McAllister and his friends are captured and taken back to Gathmara, and unless these partially-trained military cadets of C.H.A.O.S. find a way to stop the lizard-like Thules, Earth's domination is assured.
    ISBN 978-1-59554-755-2 (hardback)
    [1. Secret societies—Fiction. 2. Adventure and adventurers—Fiction. 3. Extraterrestrial beings—Fiction. 4. Supernatural—Fiction. 5. Conduct of life—Fiction. 6. Arizona—Fiction.] I. Title.
    PZ7.L5871Dom 2013
    [Fic]—dc23   2012048742

Printed in the United States of America

13 14 15 16 17 18 RRD 6 5 4 3 2 1

To my Agents of CHAOS:

Allen Arnold
Grey Arnold
Amanda Bostic
Chewbacca
Benjamin J. Grimm
Lee Hough
Daisy Hutton
Hal Jordan
Bailey Lewis
Jesse Lewis
Joshua Lewis
Kelly Lewis
Lauren Lewis
Olivia Lewis
Kathryn Mackel
LB Norton

:: CHAPTER 1 ::

olt McAlister sat on the scorched hood of a Volvo station wagon as tendrils of smoke rose from the broken land-scape all around him, melding into a gray December sky. Rose Hill, Virginia, was gone. As in wiped off the map. Entire neighborhoods were leveled. Trees were uprooted, cars over-turned, lives lost. Thousands of lives lost. There was nothing left unless you counted the portable toilets and food trucks that FEMA brought in for the search teams.

None of it seemed real. Not the body bags stacked up in the streets. Not that Colt had been recruited to fight despite the fact that he was only sixteen. Not that his parents had been mur-dered or that his best friend's dad had tried to murder him too. And especially not the warmongering aliens who had declared war on all of mankind.

He closed his eyes for a moment and wondered what it would

feel like to get a full night of sleep. Over the last few weeks training sessions started well before dawn and lasted into the evening. The CHAOS Military Academy cadets ran, lifted weights, and sparred. They spent endless hours at the shooting range and ran through scenario after scenario in the hologram rooms where three-dimensional images looked and felt real, allowing them to visit strange worlds without ever leaving campus. He was exhausted. They all were, but the stakes were too high to slow down.

Colt's stomach churned as he watched men in hard hats pull another body from the rubble. This time it was a girl, not much older than nine or ten. A tall man carried her toward the recovery center where Colt stood guard, and for a moment Colt thought he looked familiar. It was something about the way he moved, or maybe it was his olive skin.

But Colt had seen countless volunteers over the past three days, and they all had the same stunned look—lawyers, professors, accountants, housewives—it didn't matter. They walked around, eyes glassed over and shoulders slumped. It was as though they were going through the motions, unable to comprehend how something like this could happen.

Less than a month ago, a select group had known that aliens from distant worlds lived among humanity. Now everyone knew, and everyone was terrified. It didn't matter that most of the aliens were scientists and diplomats—these aliens, the Thule, had come to conquer, and they weren't going to stop until humanity was eradicated.

Colt's stomach churned as the man walked closer. The girl in his arms was so young. So frail. Her honey-blond hair fluttered in the wind, and though her neck was bent at an awkward angle,

Colt could see her empty eyes staring back at him. Her skin was a ghostly shade of white, and her crimson nightgown pooled like blood around her frail body.

The thin material couldn't fend off the December chill, but as Colt scanned the area for a blanket he realized that it didn't matter. All the blankets in the world weren't going to bring her back.

Communities up and down the Potomac River were in ruins. The death toll in Rose Hill alone was expected to reach two thousand, with five times that many in nearby Alexandria, which was only a few miles away from CHAOS Military Academy. Some estimated as many as twenty thousand were lost, but it was too early to tell.

Colt had overheard one of his instructors mentioning that the academy had escaped damage because the real target was Washington, DC, or more to the point, the president of the United States of America. It made sense. After all, between the faculty and the cadets, there were more than a thousand men and women armed with the most advanced weapons in the history of humanity. The aliens had sent a strike force, not an army, and they couldn't risk a prolonged fight and still accomplish their primary objective.

The attacks had come in the middle of the night while most of the Eastern Seaboard slumbered. Survivors said there was something that looked like a lightning storm as the portals opened and Thule gunships burst out of the sky. At least a dozen transports delivered Thule infantry to the ground, and though local authorities tried to stop them, the Thule tore across the countryside until soldiers from the 10th Mountain Division engaged them just outside Washington.

Reinforcements arrived from as far away as Fort Bragg and Shaw Air Force Base, and when the battle was over, the president held a press conference on the front steps of the White House, claiming victory. The speech was meant to inspire, but the words were hollow. Everyone knew that the Thule didn't lose. They simply disappeared back through the portals, and when they returned, humanity would need more than luck to survive. They'd need a miracle.

"There you are."

Colt turned when he heard Danielle Salazar's voice through the speakers in his battle helmet. Like the other CHAOS cadets who had been called into service, she wore an exoskeleton called a Whitlock Armor System that made her look like a modern version of a medieval knight.

Each suit cost more than a beach house on Coronado Island, but it was equipped with power cells, processors, and an operating system that enhanced speed and strength by nearly double. The ceramic plates and ballistic mesh were stronger than metal, and the entire system was sealed and temperature-controlled. A breathing apparatus filtered the air, allowing the wearer to enter toxic atmospheres with minimal risk. In a pinch it could be used underwater, but the oxygen supply only lasted ten minutes.

Danielle's helmet was equipped with auto-targeting software that linked to both her sniper rifle and her .45-caliber handgun. The technology made it hard to miss, not that she needed the help. In the few weeks that she had been training, Danielle had shown herself to be a natural marksman, rising to the top 10 percent in her class.

Here they were, sophomores in high school, and yet they

were already assigned to what the Department of Alien Affairs called an Elite Combat Squad. Each ECS had nine members: a squad leader and eight other cadets who were divided into Alpha and Bravo teams. Alpha teams typically specialized in recon while Bravo teams were the heavy gunners, but cadets trained to be interchangeable.

Their primary directive was to find and eliminate hostile alien life forms, which was why they took to calling themselves "exterminators" whenever their commanding officers weren't around. With the bulk of the military mobilized, the cadets were all that was left to sweep the evacuation sites that had been deci-mated in the attacks.

"What happened?" Danielle asked. "You were supposed to meet me at the rendezvous twenty minutes ago. Commander Webb didn't even know where you were."

Colt glanced at the heads-up display inside his visor. Accord-ing to the US Naval Observatory Master Clock, he was only sixteen minutes and thirty-two seconds late, but he got the point. He had been named leader of Phantom Squad, which meant that he was supposed to keep everyone else on task, not the other way around.

"Did you turn off your comlink or are you just ignoring us?" she pressed.

"The signal must be scrambled. All I heard was static."

"Can you hear me now?"

Colt hated it when she used that condescending tone. "Yeah, but it's probably because you're standing next to me."

Danielle placed her hands on her hips the way his mom used to do when she was upset with him. "Then find a tech and get it fixed, or Commander Webb is going to demote you and put Pierce in charge."

Though they weren't related by blood, Danielle was the sister Colt never had and the daughter his mom always wanted after giving birth to eight boys. Growing up, their families spent most vacations and major holidays together, and he was fairly certain there were more pictures of Danielle in his family scrapbooks than there were of him.

"Look, I'm sorry." His eyes drifted back to the little girl. "It's just that none of this makes sense. I mean, why the suburbs and not a military base . . . or the White House?"

"It's not like they didn't try," Danielle said. "They knocked the portico off the Lincoln Memorial and then blew the head off the statue."

"But why not assassinate the real thing?"

"Fear."

"What?"

"It's symbolic," Danielle said. "I mean, yeah, there's a good chance they could have killed the president, but in some ways this is worse. By destroying a symbol like Lincoln's statue, they made a statement . . . the same statement they made here and in Alexandria and everywhere else. They want us to know that nobody is safe— they could show up anytime, anywhere, and we can't stop them."

Colt felt a sense of hopelessness wash over him as he watched a Boeing CH-47 Chinook helicopter hover in the distance, its tandem rotors scattering debris. He hadn't thought of it that way, and as much as he wished it weren't true, Danielle was probably right. The Thule understood the power of terror, and they had used it to their advantage.

In the last week, people had stopped going to work. There was widespread looting, air traffic had been shut down, and the stock markets were closed. Armed members of the National Guard roamed the streets in riot gear as a show of force. It was meant to instill confidence, but all it did was breed more fear.

"How did everything go over on grid D?" Colt asked, changing the subject. Grid D used to be the neighborhoods surrounding Ridgeview Park. Now it was just a marker on the FEMA map. Police states. Curfews. Swift justice. Freedom was all but gone and so was the confidence that the government could protect its people.

Danielle shook her head. Even with the helmet in place, the gesture was incredibly sad. "No survivors."

"Any sign of Thule?"

"We've been through at least two hundred houses and we haven't even found a—"

Colt cringed as static blared through his speakers.

"Say again?" Danielle pressed her hand to the side of her helmet. "Where?"

"What happened?" Colt tried to adjust the volume control on the side of his helmet.

"Did anyone go near it?" she asked, then waited for a response. "Good. Tell them not to touch it. Tell them to . . . just get out of there."

"Touch what?" Colt said over the static.

"We're leaving now." Danielle started to walk away, tightening the strap that held her sniper rifle over her shoulder.

"Danielle!"

"Commander Webb said that someone spotted a Class 2

Thule fighter a couple miles from here, and he wants us to investigate."

"What about the rest of the squad?"

"They're busy."

CHAPTER 2

C olt sped through the streets in a Humvee that was built for 'rough terrain, not for a winding obstacle course of potholes, crumpled cars, and mounds of debris.

Thud. Thud. He barreled over an aluminum ladder, and his brain bounced against his skull.

"Watch out!" Danielle yelled.

Colt didn't see the cast-iron tub until it was too late. He clenched his jaw and cranked the steering wheel to the right. Tires screeched, and the engine roared as the front bumper clipped an upright piano, erupting in an explosion of wooden panels and ivory keys. He knew he should slow down, but he couldn't. Not if there was a chance that Thule were lurking nearby.

"Display GPS," he said, and a map appeared in the heads-up display inside his visor. "Show me the shortest route to the crash site."

The word CALCULATING flashed on the screen three times before a green line appeared, connecting two dots. "Turn right onto Larpin Lane in one hundred feet," an automated voice said.

"Wait, what?" Danielle said. "There's nowhere to turn."

"Why would the GPS lie?"

"Maybe because it doesn't know the streets are buried under a foot of debris."

"Turn right," the GPS repeated.

Colt jerked the steering wheel, and the Humvee shook as it rolled up a mound of plywood, beams, and Sheetrock. *Crack!* Something beneath them broke, and the tires spun until they found traction on what was left of a sofa.

"See, it was right," Colt said as the Humvee shot down a street that had been partially cleared by a bulldozer.

"Congratulations."

There was a blur of motion as a motorcycle with a sidecar cut in front of them. "What a jerk!" Danielle cried out.

"Me or him?" Colt barely had time to react, but he managed to cut the wheel hard to the left. Their Humvee shot over a curb and into a front yard.

"Colt! Tell me you see that!"

They were speeding toward a chimney that stood in a field of ash. It was all that remained of what had been a massive house, and they were on a crash course.

Colt slammed on the brakes, and the wheels locked up. Tires cut through wet grass, digging through the mud as he spun the steering wheel to the right. Momentum turned the Humvee sideways, and time seemed to slow as the chimney loomed in front of them.

Twenty feet. Ten feet. Five.

Metal crumpled as the driver's-side door slammed into the chimney. Colt felt the impact roll up his spine and into his shoulders. His head snapped to the left and then the right as bricks fell on the roof in rapid succession. One caught the windshield and left a jagged crack before it fell to the ground.

Colt hit the gas and the Humvee shot forward, rolling over a birdbath and then jumping back onto the street. From the corner of his eye he could see Danielle looking at him, and even though her face was hidden behind the helmet, he could imagine the fire in her eyes.

"Look, I'm sorry," he said. "But—"

"But what? You almost got us killed!"

"I know. It's just that . . ." Colt hesitated, trying to think of a good excuse. It didn't matter that he was only sixteen or that it had only been six months since he earned his driver's license. Not when the world needed heroes to rise above themselves.

:: CHAPTER 3 ::

The Thule were killing machines that looked like walking lizards with six arms, and their hooked teeth and clawed fingers were designed to rend flesh from bone.

Until recently most of the world thought they were little more than characters from a comic book. In the past, some, like President Franklin Delano Roosevelt, had known the truth. He'd kept their existence a secret, fearing that if people knew Hitler had joined forces with a race of shape-shifting aliens it would cause mass hysteria at a time when Americans needed stability.

He'd also hidden the existence of Project Chrysalis, a top-secret program he developed where infants were inoculated with Thule blood in an attempt to create a breed of super soldiers who could defend the United States against extraterrestrial threats. Seventy years and billions of dollars later, the project was on the verge of cancellation—until the first successful test case in recorded history was a boy from San Diego named Colt McAlister. The military finally had its savior.

"That's it!" Danielle said as she pointed at a four-story brick building surrounded by trees and rolling hills.

As they entered the parking lot they could see the tail end of the Thule fighter sticking out from the rooftop. Since it was nearly impossible for humans to speak the alien language, they had taken to classifying Thule ships using reptilian names. This particular fighter was called a Taipan, named for the most venomous snake on the planet.

"How long has it been here?" Colt asked, wondering why no one had spotted it in the initial sweep.

"I know as much as you do." Danielle opened her door, grabbed a camera out of her duffel bag, and walked toward the building.

"Wait a minute. What are you doing?" Colt said.

"What does it look like I'm doing?"

"Trying to get yourself killed." He shouldered his assault rifle and grabbed Danielle's sniper rifle. "You don't go into a hot zone without your weapon."

"So now you're worried about protocol?"

"I'm worried about one of the Thule ripping you in half."

"Right, because this place is infested. Remind me again, how many Thule have we seen over the last three days? Because I'm pretty sure the number is zero."

"That doesn't mean they aren't here."

"Fine, I'll prove it." She picked up a brick, bounced it in her palm, and threw it at the window.

"Have you lost your mind?"

Danielle shook her head. "Since none of them are rushing out to rip my head off, I'd say we're fine."

Colt could feel the hair on the back of his neck stand on end as wind whipped across the parking lot, causing a metal handicap parking sign to shake. A newspaper fluttered. Branches creaked in nearby trees, threatening to snap. But there was no sign of the Thule. Yet.

Over the last two weeks, when Colt wasn't battling replicas of Thule inside a hologram chamber, he was studying them in a classroom. He learned about their fractured political structure and how their government had splintered into five warring factions, each led by a warlord who sought supremacy over the others. He knew that four of the factions had united in the fight against humanity, and more importantly, he knew that each Thule had a jaw that was strong enough to bite Danielle in half if it got hold of her.

"Are you coming or what?" she asked. But before he could respond, Danielle walked into the lobby of the apartment building with her camera at the ready instead of her gun.

:: CHAPTER 4 ::

olt kept his finger on the trigger as the flashlights mounted to his helmet flared to life. The lobby was a shambles: over-turned desks, shattered chairs, a collapsed wall revealing an empty swimming pool wreathed by an iron fence out back.

He took one step and then another as a gust of wind sent dead leaves dancing across the hardwood floor. Something moved in the shadows, and his muscles tensed. "Danielle . . . is that you?" he said into his comlink. "Can you hear me?"

"Sorry, I'm getting a lot of static."

"Not funny."

"You're breaking up."

"Danielle."

"See you on the roof."

The elevator was out of commission, so Colt rushed up the stairwell, hoping to catch her before she ran headlong into a nest of Thule. It was times like this when he most missed Oz Romero, and not because his friend could bench-press four hundred pounds or hit a bull's-eye with a sniper rifle from three-quarters of a mile away.

Colt missed Oz's confidence, his quirky humor, and the way he always smiled—even when it felt like the world was crashing down around them. He understood why Abigail Thorne, the new superintendent of the academy, had expelled Oz when she took over, even after it looked like Oz would be able to stay, but that didn't mean he had to like it. Oz wasn't like his dad, the former director of CHAOS who had hired a Thule assassin to kill a list of US government officials—along with Colt, who he thought had wanted to remove him from his post.

Oz had testified that he didn't have anything to do with the plot, and he not only passed a series of lie detector tests to prove it, he let them take a recording of his memories. They didn't find one shred of evidence; still, Superintendent Thorne said she couldn't risk keeping him even though Colt and more than a dozen instructors had testified on his behalf.

Grandpa even spoke to the man who had assumed control of CHAOS. Ezekiel Watson was not only the Director of the Department of Alien Affairs but also an old friend. It didn't matter. Their public relations team thought that keeping Oz around would mean bad publicity at a time when the American people needed to know that they could trust their government to protect them.

Thinking about it made Colt angry. *I can't go there, not now*, he thought. *Look. Listen. Evaluate.* Do it all again and then move. He pressed forward but stopped when he heard something heavy shuffle across the floor above him.

"Colt, can you hear me?"

"Where are you?"

"I can see the ship but—" Her voice cut out.

Wood groaned as something big made its way up the stairs from behind. *I knew it,* Colt thought. *We walked right into a trap.* He turned off the flashlights as he stepped around the corner and stood with his back against the wall.

The dull thud of footsteps grew closer, and he tried to control his breathing—in through the mouth, out through the nose. He pictured the nerve clusters on a Thule. The throat. Ears. Groin. Armpits. If those didn't work, there were always the eyes.

His body tensed. The creature was close enough that he could hear it breathing. *It's now or never.* He spun around and jabbed at its throat with his rifle, but it deflected the blow. Colt followed up with a knee to the midsection, but it slipped to the side and knocked the rifle from his hands.

"Take it easy, McAlister."

"Oz?" The person standing there looked like his friend, but something was off. Thule were shapeshifters, which meant that they could take any human form. This Oz was too thin, and his cheeks were too gaunt.

"Yeah, it's me." He held up his arms in a show of surrender, but it wasn't enough.

Colt drew the .45-caliber handgun from his holster and took aim.

"What are you doing?" Oz asked.

"Prove it."

"What, you think I'm one of them?"

"You have five seconds."

"Come on, you can't be—"

"Four . . . three . . ."

"Okay. I met you at Chandler High . . . you stink at video games . . . you're in love with Lily Westcott . . . and you keep your dad's Phantom Flyer ring in your sock drawer. You happy?"

"What's my favorite *Phantom Flyer* issue?"

Oz rolled his eyes. "You tell people it's #11 because that's what it should be, but it's really #97—the first one your dad gave you."

"I almost shot you," Colt said, lowering the gun. "What are you doing here?"

Oz shrugged. "Somebody has to watch your back. Anyway, where's Danielle?"

"Taking pictures of the wreck."

"By herself?" Oz started up the last flight of stairs, but Colt grabbed him by the arm.

"Listen, about everything that happened—"

"Forget it," Oz said, cutting him off. "You didn't have anything to do with it. Besides, they didn't have a choice."

Someone screamed.

"Danielle!"

Oz grabbed Colt's assault rifle and charged up the stairs with Colt on his heels. They burst through the door and ran down the hall toward the wreck, but stopped when they saw Danielle in the clutches of a Thule.

Should I spare her life or dine on her liver?

The chilling voice was somehow inside Colt's head, like the creature was using telepathy.

"Let her go," Colt said, his gun held high.

Danielle gasped as the Thule tore her helmet away.

"I have the shot," Oz said, the barrel of the weapon pointed at the Thule's right eye.

Colt felt something like adrenaline surge through him as his thoughts gave way to instinct. He dropped the handgun and sprang forward, his lip curled back as he grabbed the Thule by its wrist and twisted. Bone snapped, and the alien dropped Danielle.

The Thule lashed out, but Colt ducked out of the way. A second strike from the Thule was followed by a third and then a fourth, but somehow Colt was too fast. He stepped to the left and then the right, countering each blow, first to its throat, then its ear, and twice to the cluster of nerves beneath its arms.

I'll suck the marrow from your bones!

The Thule spoke into his mind as Colt jumped up and brought his elbow down on its skull. Bone shattered and its eyes rolled back in its head as it crumpled to the ground, but Colt wasn't finished. He jumped on its chest, pinning two of its shoulders beneath his knees. Fury erupted as he rained down blow after blow on the alien's face. Its jaw went slack, its tongue lolled, and green blood oozed from deep cuts.

"That's enough," someone said, but the voice was far away.

Colt's nostrils flared as the fear of seeing Danielle in its clutches was replaced by hatred for the warmongering Thule who had already taken his parents. He knew they wouldn't stop until everyone he loved was eradicated.

"It's over."

The voice was closer now, but Colt ignored it. He brought his fist against the Thule's jaw, and it snapped to hang at an odd angle. Another blow, and bone tore through skin as scales and blood sprayed the floor.

"You're freaking her out."

Colt turned and saw Danielle standing with her back against the wall, tears streaming down her face, her eyes wide with fear. Oz walked over and brushed the hair from her cheek. His fingers lightly caressed her skin. He smiled gently as she wrapped her arms around his neck and buried her face in his chest, sobbing.

"I know," he said as he stroked her hair. "I know."

Colt's hands shook uncontrollably. His knuckles were covered with the same green blood that was splattered on the walls and the floor. He looked over at the Thule's broken body, and he knew why Danielle was crying. She wasn't afraid of the Thule. She was afraid of him.

:: CHAPTER 5 ::

Superintendent Thorne has changed the name of the academy," Colt said as they stood on the lawn outside the apartment building. "She's calling it the Intergalactic Defense Academy."

"As in IDA?" Oz said. "Isn't that an old lady's name?"

"Exactly," Colt said. He hesitated, knowing that they were about to part ways but wishing they didn't have to. "Look, I think you should come back with us."

"Yeah, right."

"We'll tell the superintendent what you did—that you helped save our lives."

Oz shook his head. "She thinks I went back to Arizona with my mom, remember? That was the deal. If she knew I was here, she'd have me thrown into a cell next to my dad. And she'd do the same to you."

"I'd like to see her try," Danielle said. "Maybe I'll erase her identity."

"Don't even think about it," Oz said. "You're not a criminal. Besides, she's not worth it. Neither am I."

"Whatever," Colt said. Oz couldn't have been more wrong as far as he was concerned. They needed him in the war against the Thule. Colt needed him. "You're part of our ECS. You're part of Phantom Squad."

"I appreciate it," Oz said. "I really do, but you can't worry about me now. You have bigger fish to fry, like your training. How's everything going with Project Betrayal? Is it still on track?"

"We're not ready," Colt said. "We haven't passed any of our hologram scenarios. I mean, we're not even close. Jackal, Blizzard, and Lightning have already passed, and I'm supposed to be leading the mission. What does that say about me?"

"You'll get there," Oz said. "Besides, your squad is filled with a bunch of brainiacs, not soldiers. Plus, you're stuck with Pierce. What did they expect?"

"They moved the go date to January 15."

"What?" Oz asked. "That's less than three weeks."

"Exactly," Colt said. "And it's going to fail without you."

Oz smiled as he shook his head. "Sometimes I don't get you, McAlister. Just about everyone on the planet thinks you're our only hope for survival, but you're worried about me? You got this." A helicopter flew by, and he pulled his hood over his head. "Look, it's been great and everything, but I have to go."

"Where are you staying?" Danielle asked.

"Around."

"What's that supposed to mean?"

"I've been camping out at this place that isn't too far from campus."

"Like, in a tent?" she said. "Are you trying to catch pneumonia? It's below freezing every night."

"Relax," Oz said with his easy smile. "I found a cabin stocked with enough Spam, powdered eggs, and baked beans to last for months. It even has a generator, so I can watch TV if I get bored. But I spend most of my time stalking you two."

"That's creepy," Colt said.

Oz shrugged. "Remember somebody has to watch your back."

Danielle removed her helmet, and her ponytail fell down the back of her armor. Her eyes were red and puffy, and she just stood there staring at Oz like she wanted to say something. Instead, she walked over to him, stood on her tiptoes, and kissed his cheek.

"What was that for?" he said.

She frowned.

"What?" Oz said.

She rolled her eyes. "We have to go. Just make sure you stay out of sight, okay? I don't want anything to happen to you."

"I'll be fine," he said as he brushed a strand of hair from her cheek. "Oh, and before I forget, guess who called me a couple days ago, McAlister?"

"Who?"

"Lily."

"Seriously?" Colt suddenly forgot that they were standing in the middle of a war zone. The sound of her name made his heart race. Lily Westcott was stunningly beautiful, played the guitar, and sang like an angel. But it was more than that. Behind her amazing smile was a lifetime of pain. Like Colt, she had lost both her parents, and the two of them understood each other without having to say a word.

"You realize Superintendent Hill can trace your line," Danielle said.

"It's encrypted," Oz said. "Besides, we only talked for a couple minutes."

"What did she say?" Colt said.

"You mean, did she mention you?" Oz smiled like the Cheshire cat as Colt blushed beneath his helmet. "She asked how you were doing."

Colt felt his chest constrict as he waited for Oz to say something more, but he didn't. "That was it?"

"She said that she missed you . . . Well, technically she said that she missed all of us, but I knew what she meant."

"Oh."

"And you can relax, because she's not dating anybody," Oz said.

"Really?"

"Really." Oz walked over and sat on his motorcycle. "I still have the same number," he said, showing them his smartphone. "If you need me, call." With that, he put the phone back in his pocket, pulled on a pair of driving goggles, and started the motorcycle.

||||||||||||||||||||||||||||

The drive back to the academy was quiet. Awkward. Danielle sat in the passenger's seat, her eyes focused on the barren landscape. Colt had seen her upset before, but never like this.

"If it makes you feel better, I'm going to turn myself in," he said, glancing at the rearview mirror to make sure that his skin hadn't morphed into scales or his teeth weren't pointed. "I mean, you looked pretty freaked out, and I get it. I just . . . I don't know." He took a deep breath and exhaled. "I just want you to know that I'm sorry."

Danielle turned and looked at him in a way that made him feel like a complete and total idiot. "What are you talking about?"

"You know, how I snapped back there," Colt said. "It's like it wasn't even me—or maybe it was, but that's the thing. I don't know who I am anymore. Am I human or an alien or . . ." He was afraid to say it out loud, but what if he wasn't either? What if he was alone? "Look, all I know is that something isn't right, so I'm going to let them lock me up until someone figures out what's going on, because the last thing I want to do is hurt someone I care about."

"See that?" Danielle said as they passed the charred remains of a gas station next to the off ramp. "We need you out here so that kind of stuff doesn't happen again—not locked up feeling sorry for yourself because you're different."

"I'm a freak."

"No. Different. And you always have been. Remember the time you brought me to that beach party with your friends over in Carlsbad? One minute we were roasting marshmallows around the bonfire, and the next you were gone. It took us an hour to find you, and do you know what you were doing?"

Colt shrugged.

"You were teaching a homeless guy how to play your guitar."

"Oh yeah. I forgot about that."

"We had to drag you away so we didn't miss curfew, but we were still late because you had to go back and give him your last twenty dollars and a book."

"*The Hobbit.*"

"Normal people don't do stuff like that."

"Read?"

"I'm being serious."

"Maybe, but this is different," Colt said. "It's like I can feel this living thing inside of me, and it wants to take over."

"So don't let it."

Colt wanted to tell her that it wasn't that easy, but he didn't. Danielle had always been honest with him, even when it wasn't something he wanted to hear. And more often than not she was right.

What if it was that easy? He'd been carrying the Thule DNA in his system for ten years, and it hadn't manifested until recently. Maybe it was triggered by fear or anger or even adrenaline. Maybe breathing exercises or yoga could stop it. Or maybe they could give him some kind of pill to keep the alien in check.

"I guess I just hated the way you looked at me back there," he said. "I don't want you to be scared."

"You thought I was scared of *you*?"

"More like terrified, but yeah."

"No," she said, shaking her head. "That thing came out of nowhere. I honestly thought I was going to die without being able to say good-bye to my parents or you or . . ." She covered her eyes as they misted over. "I'm sorry, it's just that Oz didn't answer my e-mails, and I couldn't text him because I thought his phone was disconnected." She wiped away a tear as it streamed down her cheek. "I was scared that he was going to go out and do something stupid to prove that he isn't like his dad. I mean, I'd hold my breath every time one of the rescue teams found a body, because I thought it was going to be him—and then he just shows up and tells us that he's been here all the time? He's such a jerk!"

Colt sat there, not sure what to say or if he should say anything at all. On one hand, he was relieved that she wasn't scared of him, but then again, he hated to see her so upset. He'd known there was a spark between Oz and Danielle from the moment he first saw them together, and he figured they'd eventually announce that they were dating, but this was different. It was deeper. Real. It was love.

Danielle sniffled as she wiped her eyes and straightened her ponytail. "Just so we're on the same page—if you tell anyone about this conversation, you're a dead man."

"My lips are sealed."

"And when we get back, you're going to see a doctor. Period."

:: CHAPTER 6 ::

By the time they got back to campus, Colt's body ached and his eyes were heavy and all he wanted was to go back to his dorm room and sleep, but Danielle grabbed him by the arm and started walking him to the infirmary.

"What about my report?" he said.

"It can wait," she said. "Besides, we already called it in. Let the investigators handle it."

"Tell that to my commanding officer."

A girl approached wearing one of the new Intergalactic Defense Academy uniforms. It was formfitting, like neoprene, and it had the IDA crest and orange striping that signified she was part of Jackal Squad.

"Don't look now, but I think Miranda's trying to get your attention," Danielle said, rolling her eyes.

"Sure she is," Colt said.

Miranda Patel was widely considered the most beautiful girl on campus. Whenever she was around, the male cadets stopped and stared. It didn't matter if she was walking, running, or eating an apple; it was like she had super-powered pheromones that hypnotized the opposite sex. Then again, it could have been her enormous brown eyes, full lips, dark skin, and that long black hair that bounced with each step she took.

"Hi," she said as she walked past them.

"Um . . . hi," Colt said with his voice caught in his throat. She smiled, and without realizing what he was doing, Colt turned and watched her walk away.

"You might want to put your tongue back in your mouth," Danielle said.

"What?" Colt turned back around and ran his hand over the stubble of his shaved head.

"Could you be any more obvious?"

"I don't know what you're talking about."

"Sure you don't."

Danielle stayed at the medical facility long enough to make sure he checked in before she left to take a shower and get something to eat. He sat in the waiting room and stared at the floor, wondering why his appointment was with someone named Dr. Roth instead of the medical team that had been monitoring him since he arrived at the campus.

Twenty minutes later a door opened, and a white robot on track wheels entered the room. It was roughly the size of a minifridge, with a red cross on its chest, a wide rectangular head, and two of its eight retractable arms fully extended.

"This way, if you please," the medibot said in a synthesized voice. A series of eyes lit up as it wheeled back around and led Colt down a hallway. It passed the examination rooms and stopped at an elevator.

"Where are we going?" Colt asked as he entered the elevator.

"Dr. Roth maintains an office on sublevel three."

"Sublevel three? Wait, what happened to Dr. Cornelius?"

"He is currently indisposed . . . Mind your fingers. Some of our subjects are a bit aggressive," it said as the doors opened.

Three other medibots were in a room that was about as big as a fast food restaurant, each one of them attending to a variety of caged animals. Their domed heads sat on top of tapered bodies that were wider at the base than they were near their shoulder joints. Their retractable arms and the cluster of eyes reminded Colt of the creepy mechanical spiders that had attacked him back at Greg's Comics in Arizona.

The walls were lined with cages made of thick glass. One held a chimpanzee that simply sat there, staring at him. Another had a nervous dog that paced back and forth, its tail swishing as it yapped. But most were filled with strange creatures.

The first thing that stood out was an enormous green slug resting in the branches of a tree like a length of gelatinous intestine. According to the plaque it was called a Storaab and was from the jungles of Gathmara, the home world of the Thule, but Colt hadn't run into any during his training scenarios in the hologram rooms. He stood there, entranced by how disgusting yet fascinating it was. The only light in its cage emanated from its body, where a complicated network of veins was lit up like a neon sign beneath translucent skin.

Nearby, colorful reptiles called Kyax fed on a carcass. One

tossed a hunk of marbled flesh into the air and snatched it in its jaws as its leathery wings pounded the air. The Finopod in the adjacent cage looked like a Venus flytrap, but it was nearly as tall as Colt. And he recognized monkey-like creatures called Twilek as they glided from a platform to a series of poles, using membranes that ran from wrist to ankle like those of flying squirrels. It was incredible to see them in the flesh instead of as a holographic representation.

"Interesting, aren't they?"

Colt turned to see a man with the beginnings of a goatee and hair that hung down to his shoulders. He was in good enough shape that his tight black T-shirt didn't look too ridiculous, and most of his right arm was covered in an intricate series of tattoos.

"Sorry," Colt said. "I, um . . . I was looking for Dr. Roth."

"Then you're in the right place," the man said. "You must be Cadet McAlister."

"Dr. Roth?"

"In the flesh."

"Are you a veterinarian or something?"

"Not exactly," Dr. Roth said. "Though I do know a thing or two about Thule physiology. In fact, you might say I wrote the book on the subject." He stood there like he was expecting applause, but Colt just stared at him. "Anyway, given the unusual nature of your condition, I've been asked to take over your medical care."

"What about Dr. Cornelius?"

"He'll still be part of the team, but in more of an advisory role."

"Does my grandpa know about this?"

"We had lunch yesterday," Dr. Roth said as he pulled a penlight from his pocket. "He's quite the storyteller. May I?" He pried Colt's eyelid apart without waiting for a response and shined the light at his retina. "When did you first notice that your eyes had turned color?"

"I don't know . . . a few weeks ago, I guess."

"Fascinating. And you haven't noticed any other physical manifestations? Scales? Protrusions? The start of a tail?"

"No."

"What about your emotional state? Do you have extreme mood shifts?"

"Not really."

"What about fits of crying? Hopelessness? Anger?"

"Sometimes," Colt said. "The anger part anyway—like today when I thought a friend was in trouble. Something snapped, and the next thing I know I'm covered in blood, my knuckles are raw, and the Thule is lying there not moving."

"How did that make you feel?"

"I don't know," Colt said. "Scared, I guess. I mean, what if something happens and I turn on someone I care about?"

"That's certainly a fair question, though I wonder if it has more to do with the stress you're under. I can't imagine what it must feel like to have the weight of the entire world on your shoulders. It can't be easy."

Colt averted his eyes. He knew Dr. Roth was talking about Project Betrayal and how because Colt had blood from a Thule coursing through his veins, people actually thought he was part of an ancient prophecy that would destroy the Thule and save humanity. Just thinking about it sounded laughable . . . and yet maybe it was true. Maybe this was the plan God had for him all along.

"I want you to be honest with me," Colt said.

"I'll do my best."

"Do you think I'm turning into one of them?"

"The Thule?" Dr. Roth asked as he started chewing the inside of his cheek. "If it's honesty you're after, then I'd have to say that I have my doubts. After all, you've been carrying their DNA for the better part of ten years, and the only physical manifestation has been your eye color, right?"

"Yeah," Colt said, which was the truth. What he didn't say was that he had heard the Thule speak inside his mind.

"Still, you're the first of your kind, which means we won't know until it happens—if it happens. All we can do for now is watch and wait."

"I was thinking that maybe they should lock me up just in case."

"That might be a bit extreme—at least for now. But I appreciate the thought. It shows your character." Dr. Roth walked over to a bank of drawers and pulled out a needle and syringe. "Would you mind if I took a blood sample?"

"Do I have a choice?"

"You always have a choice."

Colt closed his eyes and held out his arm, and Dr. Roth tied a piece of medical tubing just above his elbow. Colt had never been a fan of needles, and if Dr. Roth was going to stick him, then he didn't want to watch.

"There we are," the doctor said. "Now this may pinch."

Colt felt something hit his arm, but there wasn't any pain.

When he opened his eyes, Dr. Roth was standing there looking at a needle that was bent at odd angles.

"That was unexpected," the doctor said.

"What happened?"

"I'm not exactly sure." Dr. Roth placed the needle into a disposal container. "Let's try that again." He slammed the second needle into Colt's arm like he was trying to drive a nail through a board, and once again it crumpled.

:: CHAPTER 7 ::

A s Colt left the lab, he wondered if Dr. Roth had already filed his report and how long it would take before a team of Black Ops agents threw a bag over his head and stuffed him in the back of a van where they would whisk him away to a secret facility and experiment on him until they found a way to re-create his new armored skin.

He thought about what kind of gas they would use to knock him out, since they couldn't exactly hit him with a dart; how long it would last; and whether or not he would be strong enough to break the bindings that would no doubt be wrapped around his wrists and ankles.

As he rounded a corner, he saw an armed DAA agent in winter camouflage, complete with a ski mask and goggles, and he stopped. The guard looked at him, and Colt felt like a piglet looking at the jaws of a wolf. He glanced over his shoulder to see if there was a second guard sneaking up behind him with the hood, but he couldn't see anyone. His eyes went to the bushes and then the trees, knowing there had to be an agent with a smoke grenade or something that would knock him out.

It was freezing outside, and his nose started to run. He swiped at it with the back of his sleeve, and that's when he saw Miranda Patel and a group of her friends walking toward him, the chatter of their voices out of place in a gloomy world shrouded by the threat of annihilation at the hands of alien invaders. In the back of his mind he could hear Danielle telling him not to stare at her, which was much easier said than done, but right now his focus was on trying to get away.

Colt took advantage of the distraction. There was no way anyone would try to abduct him with so many witnesses around, so he walked toward the girls, trusting that would give him enough time to make it to the commissary, where he hoped to find Danielle.

The DAA agent was watching each step that he took, but as he approached the girls, his thoughts shifted from fear to a self-conscious awkwardness. These girls were not just beautiful, they were breathtaking. And Miranda stood out above them all.

Colt was suddenly aware that a string of clear snot was running down his lip, and his tongue shot out to lick it away. Embarrassed, he stopped and sniffed, but he had to wipe it with his sleeve again. Miranda must not have noticed because she smiled, and before he could stop himself he raised his hand and wiggled his fingers. *I'm such an idiot.*

"Hi." Her voice was rich and sweet, almost musical.

"Hey," he replied, his voice cracking.

"I don't think we've officially met, but I'm Miranda." She extended her hand, and Colt just stared at it. Danielle and her friend Stacy had both cut their nails short like most of the other girls at the academy, but Miranda's fingernails were perfectly manicured.

Slowly, cautiously, he reached out and took her hand, painfully aware that his palms were sweating. Her smile widened, and as his skin touched hers, his heart started to flutter like a speed bag in a boxing gym. "Um, Colt. I mean . . . I'm Colt. Colt McAlister."

"Yeah, I know," she said as the other girls laughed. "I saw you earlier today, over by the infirmary. Everything okay?"

"Yeah," Colt said. "Fine. I'm fine. Couldn't be better. It was just a normal checkup. You know, where they check your reflexes and your heart rate and stuff. No big deal." Colt bit his lower lip in an attempt to keep from babbling any more nonsense, but at least she didn't know about his secret identity as a mutant human with alien DNA coursing through his veins.

"That's good," Miranda said. "I mean, that you're fine."

"You look fine too," Colt said, and the moment the words left his lips his eyes shot wide. "I meant that you look healthy, not that you're fine. Not that you aren't attractive, because you are, but . . ." Colt stood there, unable to shut his mouth. He felt like he was in a car and not only were the brake lines cut but he was heading for a cliff. "Look, I'm sorry."

Miranda broke into a wide smile. "You're not bad yourself," she said in a way that made Colt's fingers and toes feel like they were tingling.

"So . . . ah . . . are you going to class or something?" He knew his face was more than likely the brightest shade of red imaginable.

"Actually, we're going to the shooting range," Miranda said. "I just finished my certification on the SK-14, and today I'm going to be on the Satterfield S80."

"The Widowmaker?"

"You don't think I can handle it?" She raised a single eyebrow and placed her hands on her hips as though inviting Colt to judge her based on her physique. His face grew an even darker shade of red. He knew that he shouldn't look, but the allure was overwhelming.

Miranda's curves were on full display in the tight uniform. He knew that she was watching him, but he couldn't stop looking until Danielle's voice invaded his thoughts. *You realize that she's somebody's daughter, not a piece of meat. Right?*

"No. I'm sure you can," Colt said, fumbling to gain control of his thoughts and his hormones.

"Bailey and Lauren are going for their S70 certification, and Olivia is testing on the NT-7," Miranda said. "You know, the pulse rifle."

"Impressive."

"When she gets it, our whole squad will be certified," Miranda said. "Anyway, I was hoping that I'd get a chance to talk to you." She hesitated and looked at her friends before she turned back to Colt. "We heard about the book."

"Oh," he said, confused about which book but not wanting to sound ignorant.

"I can't believe they're going to make it into a movie."

"Yeah, me either."

"You have no idea what we're talking about, do you?" Miranda asked.

"Not exactly."

"That's so cute."

Colt blushed.

"They're making your biography into a movie," she said.

"Wait, what?"

"Someone wrote an unauthorized biography about you, and a studio bought the movie rights. They hired a screenwriter and everything."

"Look, I'm sorry, but I'm late and I . . . um . . . have to get going." Colt figured it was just a rumor. Why would anyone want to make a movie about him? Especially with the world falling apart. Making a movie—any movie—seemed so meaningless.

"What are you doing for lunch?" Miranda asked.

"I don't know."

"Maybe we could sit together."

"Yeah, maybe." Colt cut across the lawn, frost crunching beneath his boots as he tried to make sense of what just happened. Miranda hadn't said a word to him since they arrived, and suddenly she wanted to sit with him at lunch? Maybe she was a shape-shifting assassin sent to take him out. Or maybe he was losing his mind.

He passed the bronze statue of the Phantom Flyer, who also happened to be his grandfather, Murdoch McAlister. Colt was about to head into the commissary when he saw a group of cadets from Blizzard, Lightning, Anvil, and a few other squads, so he dashed across the lawn to see what was going on.

Fighting was part of the curriculum at the CHAOS Military Academy, but brawling outside of class was strictly forbidden. Still, curiosity trumped his hunger, and he headed over to see who was stupid enough to risk cleaning the public restrooms with a toothbrush. He stopped when he saw the first combatant.

"Jonas?"

Jonas Hickman was short, plump, incredibly shy, and quite possibly the most intelligent person—faculty included—on the entire campus. He graduated from the Georgia Institute of Technology with a degree in computer science when he was only twelve and got his master's in robotics from Carnegie Mellon University the day before his fourteenth birthday. He had been brought to CHAOS not to learn how to fight on the front lines but as part of the team working on advanced weapons systems, and even though he had been assigned to Phantom Squad, he wasn't much of a fighter. But when Colt saw who was standing across from him, it all made sense.

"Let me see your ring, Hiccup," Pierce Bowen said with his familiar sneer.

Jonas cleared his throat and pushed his glasses up off the end of his nose. "It's Hickman."

"Whatever. Just let me see it." Pierce grabbed him by the wrist and ripped the ring from Jonas's finger. "I mean, we're on the same squad, right? We're supposed to share stuff."

"Please," Jonas said. "It's . . . it's . . ."

"It's what?" Pierce said.

"An heirloom."

"Since when is a stupid Phantom Flyer ring an heirloom?"

"Give it to me!" Jonas lunged for the ring, but Pierce swept the other boy's leg out from under him and he fell.

"Leave him alone." Stacy Watson pushed through the crowd and planted herself directly in front of Pierce.

Like Pierce and Jonas, she was a member of Phantom Squad. Her ginger hair was pulled back in a ponytail, and she had skin the color of flour with a smattering of freckles that dusted her nose. She was also the first girl Colt had met who actually knew as much about the Phantom Flyer as he did, and between that and her emerald eyes, he was intrigued.

"Or what?" Pierce said, crossing his arms.

Stacy shook her head. "You're supposed to have his back. Never mind the fact that he's working on the prototype for a weapon that could take out a Thule carrier. So, yeah, I can see why beating him up makes so much sense."

Pierce narrowed his eyes and took a step toward her, his fists clenched.

"Hitting her is only going to make things worse." Colt walked over and helped Jonas to his feet. His skin was rough like a lizard's or a shark's, which was strange considering that Jonas didn't exactly use his hands for physical labor.

"Stay out of it," Pierce said. "Besides, we were only messing around."

"Give him the ring," Stacy said.

"I tell you what," Pierce said. "I'll give it to *you* for a kiss."

"Not a chance." Stacy snatched the ring away and handed it to Jonas.

"We used to do a lot more than kiss," Pierce said.

Stacy spun on her heels, eyes narrow and face red with anger. "Don't."

"What's wrong, you don't want your new boyfriend to hear about how you like to—"

She slapped him across the face, and there was a moment

when the only sound was the flag above the commissary snap-ping in the wind.

Pierce smiled, and his tongue went to the corner of his mouth in search of blood. "McAlister can have you," he said, as though she was his to give away. "But you know he's one of them, right? They shot him up with Thule blood to try and turn him into some kind of super soldier."

Colt's heart started to race. How did Pierce know? Danielle wouldn't have told him, and Dr. Roth was supposed to be bound by doctor-patient confidentiality.

Pierce's father.

Senator Bowen was head of the Senate's Committee on National Intelligence, which meant he had access to military records—including secret experimental programs. Those same reports would explain how Colt had gained over fifteen pounds of muscle mass in the last three weeks. That he was stronger. Faster. That his reflexes were uncanny and his skin as resistant as Kevlar.

"Come on," Pierce said, taunting him. "Show us how you can shape-shift."

:: CHAPTER 8 ::

What seems to be the problem?"

Everyone turned to see Captain James Starling, the director of the CHAOS Military Academy's flight training program, and an Arconian named Giru Ba, who was one of his assistant instructors. Starling was handsome, or at least he could have been if he hadn't let himself go. His hair was thick, his shoulders broad, and his jaw square, but his waistline had expanded and his eyes were bloodshot either from lack of sleep or from too many long nights at a local pub. Giru Ba, on the other hand, was tall and elegant, with skin the color of sea foam, enormous eyes, and what looked like a curved beak in place of lips.

"I'm not witnessing fisticuffs, am I?" Starling asked, raising a single eyebrow. "And both of you from the same squad?"

Giru Ba stood placidly behind him, her eyes unblinking.

"No, sir," Jonas said, placing his glasses back onto his face at an odd angle.

"Then what, may I ask, were you doing on the ground?"

"Pierce was . . . well . . ."

"Yes?"

"He was just showing me a new fighting technique, that's all."

"Is that true?" Captain Starling asked.

"Yeah," Pierce said.

"I wasn't talking to you," Captain Starling said. "I was talking to Cadet McAlister."

Colt looked at Jonas, who was staring at the ground. "I guess," he said.

"Then that's good enough for me." Captain Starling turned to face the cadets, who looked more than a little disappointed that they weren't going to see a fight. "Now, off with the lot of you before I decide to give you all a demerit."

"A demerit?" Jonas said.

"Let it go." Stacy took him by the arm and led him toward the library.

"Not you," Captain Starling said as Colt started to walk away.

"Sir?" He closed his eyes, waiting for whatever bad news was about to follow.

"The president believes that the country—in fact, the world—needs a shot of hope in these dark days. He wants to resurrect the Phantom Flyer and his Agents of CHAOS."

"Grandpa?"

"No, son, not your grandfather. He's much too old for the rigors that lie ahead."

Colt looked over to Giru Ba, hoping she would tell him that this was all a joke, but she just stood there. "Then who?"

"Isn't it obvious? The president has picked you."

Colt's first thought was that the president wanted him to dress up in a costume and fly around in a jet pack looking for criminals—which, given that the world was at war with a race of aliens who wanted to exterminate humanity, seemed ridiculous, particularly in light of Project Betrayal. In less than three weeks he was supposed to lead a covert team through a portal and into Dresh, the capital city of the Thule. He didn't have time to play superhero.

The truth was even worse.

"Think of it as a traveling air show that's part Blue Angels, part Broadway musical. Are you ready for the title?"

"Not really."

"It's called *Phantasmic . . . March to Victory!*" Captain Starling spread his fingers wide, and his arms shot into the air like a burst of fireworks.

"Seriously?"

"Wait until you see the promotional posters. They're amazing, don't you think?"

"Extraordinarily so," Giru Ba said with a slight nod.

Colt stood there, dumbstruck, as Captain Starling explained how Colt would play the part of the Phantom Flyer and team up with his Agents of CHAOS to fight actors who would be dressed as Thule. He pulled up some pictures of the costumes on a tablet computer, and all Colt could think about was how they looked like extras from a rejected episode of *Power Rangers*.

"There's going to be pyrotechnics and smoke machines and

a chorus line and . . ." Captain Starling finally took a breath. "I wanted to surprise you with this, but I can't keep it in any longer. The National Symphony Orchestra is going to play an original score by the composer who wrote the soundtrack for *Star Wars*. Can you believe it?"

"That's great," Colt said, distracted by the tsunami of questions raging in his head. "But what about . . . you know?"

"You're referring to Project Betrayal, is that it?" Captain Starling asked, the smile never fading from his lips.

Colt looked over his shoulder to make sure that no one was listening. After all, despite the fact that everyone had to submit to daily testing to make sure shape-shifting Thule hadn't infiltrated the campus, it was hard to trust anyone.

"The president and I are fully aware of your responsibilities, as are Superintendent Thorne and your grandfather," Captain Starling said in a way that made it sound like he was on equal footing with the president of the United States. "I'll admit that we've had to juggle a few things to make the schedule work, but we feel you're young enough to handle it."

"Meaning what, I'm skipping sleep?"

"Not skipping—at least not exactly. You know, they say Thomas Jefferson only slept four hours a night. Or was that Abraham Lincoln? He was the one who hunted vampires, as I recall." Captain Starling shrugged. "No matter. With modern medicine, sleep has practically become unnecessary."

"I don't even get four hours now."

"What a sense of humor!" Captain Starling laughed.

"It would be wise to get plenty of rest tonight," Giru Ba said. "Captain Starling has scheduled your first practice at 0400 hours."

"As in the morning?"

Captain Starling laughed even louder as he slapped Colt on the back. "Just wait until you see your armor. It's amazing! In fact, we asked the design team at Whitlock Global to make a replica suit for the Phantom Flyer exhibit over at the library. You're going to love it!"

:: CHAPTER 9 ::

O 400 hours.

Colt stood in one of the tunnels beneath Tesla Stadium looking out at the airfield where Captain Starling was instructing a film crew. He couldn't hear what they were saying because a team of groundskeepers was mowing the grass, which was somehow lush and green despite the freezing temperatures.

"Did you see all those Secret Service agents walking around campus this morning?"

Colt turned around as a pair of second-year cadets in armored flight suits walked into the staging area, each tall and heroic, just like the Agents of CHAOS in the comic books.

"Yeah, what was up with that?" the other cadet said.

The first shrugged. "Maybe the president is coming to watch us practice or something. Think he'll take a picture with me for my Facebook page?"

It wasn't long before more of the cadets arrived in their flight suits, including three members of Phantom Squad. Stacy Watson looked like she was still asleep; Grey Arnold, one of Colt's roommates, couldn't stop smiling; and Glyph Gundar, a Fimorian, simply looked lost.

A few months ago aliens had been little more than a figment of Colt's imagination, but now they had almost become commonplace. At least eight faculty members at the academy were from other planets, and he had heard that more than a hundred of the cadets were aliens as well. Still, Glyph stood out. He was almost eight feet tall and cartoonishly thin, with gray skin, a hairless head, and enormous black eyes that dominated his narrow face.

"This is quite the spectacle, wouldn't you say, Cadet Colt McAlister?" Glyph asked when he spotted Colt standing alone at the edge of the tunnel.

"More like a total waste of time."

Glyph frowned. "I don't understand. You should be honored to continue your grandfather's legacy as the Phantom Flyer."

"I should be training in one of the simulation chambers," Colt said. "We all should."

"According to a recent Gallup poll, 65 percent of all Americans over the age of thirteen believe that the Phantom Flyer is the key to our victory over the Thule," Glyph said.

"It's called false hope," Colt said. "If we don't find a way to shut down the gateway before it's fully operational, we're all going to die."

"Perhaps. But false hope is better than no hope at all."

"Anyone else from Phantom Squad get picked?" Colt asked, half expecting to see Oz walk through the door.

"Not to my knowledge," Glyph said. "Although Cadet Danielle Salazar may have mentioned something about a control booth."

But they picked Stacy? Colt thought as he watched her sip on an energy drink. She could barely fly in a straight line, so how was she going to fly in formation? It didn't make sense.

She must have caught him staring at her, because she suddenly smiled. He smiled back. He wanted to go over and talk to her, but he wasn't sure what to say. For some reason he felt awkward around her. Stacy was great, but he wasn't ready to give up on Lily—at least not yet.

"Ah, there you are."

Colt turned to see Captain Starling walking down the tunnel toward him, eyes bright and teeth brighter.

"So what do you think about the uniform? Not bad, if I do say so myself."

"Yeah, it's great."

The original Phantom Flyer costume didn't offer much in the way of protection. It consisted of a flight suit, a bomber jacket, a pair of gloves, and a leather mask with aviator goggles. Whitlock Global had designed the new costume, which was a cross between the original and one of their armor systems. Under any other circumstances Colt would have loved it, but he felt like a fraud. No matter what Captain Starling or anyone else said, there was only one Phantom Flyer—Murdoch McAlister.

Captain Starling directed everyone to watch a display screen that covered most of an entire wall, where he showed a series of stunts using animated characters that looked like something out of a video game. It reminded Colt of the air shows that his dad used to take him to when he was younger. Squadrons of F/A-18 Hornets would do maneuvers like loops and barrel rolls, but there was an important difference: those pilots had trained together for years, while the cadets had only been flying for a few months.

"We'll start nice and slow," Captain Starling said as he led them through the tunnel and onto the aerial field. "Nothing fancy, just a simple V formation. Colt will take the point and everyone else will fall in behind him." He looked directly at Colt. "Think you can handle that?"

Colt nodded.

"Then let's fire up!" Captain Starling stepped out of the way as they put on their helmets and ignited their jet packs. Streams like flames erupted from the engines, leaving scorch marks on the ground. Almost as one, they lifted off, rising into the dark sky. Colt, however, released the throttle too quickly and shot past everyone.

"That's a bit aggressive, don't you think?" he heard Captain Starling say through the speakers in his helmet. "Now slow it down and let's take it to five hundred feet."

Colt glanced over his shoulder to see where the other pilots were, but at that speed an act as simple as turning his head changed his trajectory. He banked hard to the left, but the other pilots were skilled enough to follow without crashing into each other.

"Use the mirrors in your goggles," Captain Starling said. "That's what they're there for."

For the first time Colt noticed tiny rearview mirrors that allowed him to see reflections of the pilots as they flew behind him. They had split into a perfect V formation, each one keeping perfect pace as Colt led them in a wide loop around the stadium.

He felt his spirits rise. There was something freeing about flight, and for a moment he closed his eyes and let the cold winter air rush over him.

Captain Starling instructed them on new formations, including a barrel roll. Colt banked to the right, his arms tight to his body and his ankles crossed to keep his legs from pulling apart. As he sliced through the air, he wondered if this was what a drill bit felt like as it tore into a wall.

"This is awesome!" Grey yelped into his microphone as feedback reverberated through Colt's speakers like a herd of screeching cats.

"Are the invaders ready?" Captain Starling asked.

"Roger that." It was Danielle.

"Then let's see what we've got."

The ground shook as a massive door in the center of the grassy field started to open. Smoke issued out, and Colt watched as a platform carrying what looked like Thule fighters rose from the darkness. "Is that what I think it is?"

"Yeah, it's a Class 2 Taipan," Grey said. "But there's no way that thing is real."

"Agreed, Cadet Grey Arnold. It must be a hologram," Glyph said.

"I can assure you that it's quite real," Captain Starling said. "In fact, it was discovered in a field not far from campus."

The glass canopy above the cockpit opened, and Colt felt a spike in adrenaline as a Thule crawled out of the ship and onto the platform. More Thule rushed out from the tunnels surrounding the field, and Colt genuinely wondered if they were under attack until he saw the wires that connected their arms and the seams where their masks overlapped the rest of their costumes.

"We'll have a live orchestra for the show, but this is the actual soundtrack," Captain Starling said as orchestral music blared through the speakers.

Colt watched as the Thule formed a wide circle in the center of the field and started to dance, feet stomping, arms waving, and heads bobbing up and down and back and forth. Their forked tongues bounced against their jagged teeth.

"That's just weird," Stacy said.

"It will all make more sense once you understand the entire narrative," Captain Starling said. "Cadet Salazar?"

"Yes, Captain?"

"Is IVAN online?"

"Roger that."

"Who's Ivan?" Colt said.

"Launching in three . . ."

"Hello?"

"Two . . ."

"Is somebody going to tell me what's going on?"

"One!"

A sound like a rocket launching into space filled the sky, and Colt spun to see a red streak flying toward him from the horizon. He hovered in place, confused, until he saw the red Armored Flight Suit with the golden sickle and hammer on its chest. "No way," he said. "That's the AFS worn by that Russian guy in *The Phantom Flyer* #162. What was his name again?"

"Ivan Medvedev," Stacy said. "Code name, the Crimson Bear."

"Unfortunately Comrade Medvedev is retired, so I asked Cadet Bowen to take his place," Captain Starling said as the armor's eyes pulsed with amber light. "Prepare for evasive action."

Colt opened up his throttle and shot backward as Pierce tore past him. The AFS was ten feet tall and had to be going at least seventy miles an hour, if not faster.

"I thought that reenacting a scene from one of the Phantom Flyer comic books would be the perfect way to introduce you to the world," Captain Starling said.

"Incoming!"

Pierce rushed toward him, the red paint of his AFS shining bright beneath the stadium lights. Flames erupted from the thrusters, and he reached out with an enormous armored hand and took Colt by the throat.

"A little . . . help," Colt said as he struggled to breathe.

"That's enough," Captain Starling said, but Pierce didn't let go. "Cadet Bowen!"

With a flick of his wrist, Pierce tossed Colt to the side. "This is the hero who's supposed to save us from the Thule? Give me a break."

CHAPTER 10

Captain Starling ambushed Colt after practice.

"Not bad up there today," he said. "Not bad at all. Of course, practice went a bit long, so you won't have time for makeup, but that shouldn't—"

"Makeup?" Colt asked.

"Trust me, I know. You're going to look washed out, but there isn't much we can do about that now. We're already running late." Captain Starling took him by the elbow and led him into a room that wasn't much bigger than a closet.

Colt recognized the reporter from one of the twenty-four-hour news stations, but he couldn't remember if it was CNN, FOX, or MSNBC. The man was tall and slender, and his skin was an unnatural orange that could no doubt be blamed on the makeup that Captain Starling had been fretting over. He wore a dark suit with a red tie and copious amounts of cologne.

"That's him?" The cameraman asked the question loudly enough that Colt could hear.

Not that Colt blamed him. He would have expected more too. Superheroes were supposed to be tall and have a commanding personality that oozed confidence.

"What's going on?" Colt was suddenly aware of the fact that he hadn't taken a shower, and he was fairly sure that he had forgotten deodorant.

"The first of many interviews," Captain Starling said, slapping him on the back as though it were good news. "You've become a bit of a sensation, but we're going to make you into a global icon. You'll be bigger than Elvis, the Beatles, and Michael Jackson combined. Justin Bieber will want your autograph, and Lady Gaga is going to have Phantom Flyer posters hanging in her bedroom."

After the interview Colt had enough time to gulp down a protein shake before he caught up with the rest of Phantom Squad for a training session in one of the simulator rooms. The advanced hologram tech allowed the staff to run cadets through actual battle scenarios without the threat of death, thanks to a fail-safe mechanism, but in the advanced levels, injuries weren't only possible, they were common.

He wasn't surprised to find Glyph and Grey already there, telling everyone about their first day as Agents of CHAOS.

"You realize that you're not actually superheroes, right?" Pierce said.

"I'm afraid you've been given bad information, Cadet Pierce

Bowen," Glyph replied. "The United States government has officially designated each of us as an active-duty superhero. We were even given identification cards."

"Congratulations." Pierce's sarcasm was lost on Glyph, who bowed his head in recognition of what he thought was an actual compliment.

"Good morning, ladies and gentlemen." Agent Daniel O'Keefe, who was better known to the cadets as the Gamemaster, stepped onto the platform just outside the control room. He was short and stout with unusually broad shoulders, a paunch, and stubble that ran over his cheeks despite the fact that all personnel at the Intergalactic Defense Academy were supposed to be clean-shaven. "The good Lord has seen fit to bless us with another day. Good morning," he said with his Irish brogue, "and I'll be darned if I'm going to waste it. In fact, I have a special treat for you."

"We get to take a nap?" Ethan said, earning laughter from the rest of the squad.

"I'm afraid not," O'Keefe said. "As you know, we're sending the sorry lot of you to the jungles of Gathmara in less than three weeks as part of Project Betrayal, and we fully expect you to complete the mission despite your abysmal performance in the simulation chambers so far."

"Nice pep talk," Pierce said under his breath.

"What was that, Cadet Bowen?"

"Nothing, sir."

"That's what I thought." Agent O'Keefe glared at Pierce for a long moment before he turned back to the rest of the squad. "What you might not know is that we have an advance team on the ground just outside of Dresh right now, working with the Soldiers of the Grail. Now who can tell me why that's important?"

Glyph raised his hand.

"Yes, Cadet Gundar?"

"Five warlords representing five separate armies rose to power after the fall of the Thule government, and each warlord declared himself to be the rightful leader of their people. The Soldiers of the Grail are one of those five armies, and they are the only remaining army to stand in opposition to Aldrich Koenig and his Defense Corps."

"At least one of you has been paying attention in class," Agent O'Keefe said.

"Thank you," Glyph said.

"So we have the Soldiers of the Grail and the Defense Corps, and their hatred for one another runs deep," Agent O'Keefe said. "Can anyone other than Cadet Gundar name the other armies?"

There was a long pause before Jonas sheepishly raised his hand.

"Cadet Hickman?"

"The Dagon Alliance, the Vril, and the Black Sun Militia."

"Excellent." Agent O'Keefe pulled what looked like a remote control from a pouch on his belt and entered a series of commands that resulted in a hologram of a flag appearing in the middle of the room. "Each of the five armies has its own bloody symbol, and if you have half a brain you'll memorize which is which."

"What's the difference?" Pierce said. "They all want to kill us."

"Are you sure about that?" O'Keefe said.

Pierce narrowed his eyes as though trying to distinguish if that was an actual question. "Yeah, I'm sure."

"Has anyone heard the expression that 'the enemy of my enemy is my friend'?" The instructor scowled as he waited for a response. "Anyone?" He shook his head when Colt and Danielle were the only two cadets who raised a hand. "It means that we have something in common with the Soldiers of the Grail—we both want to take out Aldrich Koenig and his Defense Corps."

"Are you saying we made an alliance with the Thule?" Pierce asked, his defiance not lost on the other cadets.

"That's exactly what I'm saying," Agent O'Keefe said. "Which leads me to my little surprise. I'd like to introduce you to Agent Rhane, a DAA field operative who has spent most of the last decade on the ground on Gathmara."

"Does my father know about this?" Pierce said.

"Yes, he does. As does the president," Agent O'Keefe said. He walked over and rapped on the window with his knuckles, waving for a man to join him on the platform.

Agent Rhane was around six feet tall, and despite the fact that he looked like he was pushing sixty years old, he was built like a gymnast. His black hair was flecked with gray, especially around the temples, and he wore a patch over his left eye.

"Tell me this is a joke," he said with a slight southern twang, though it was hard to pinpoint which state the accent was from.

"This is it," O'Keefe said in a way that made it sound like he was just as disappointed.

"Were we ever that young?" Rhane asked.

"Afraid so."

Pierce raised his hand, but he didn't wait for anyone to call on him. "You're one of them, aren't you." It was an accusation, not a question.

"What makes you say that, Cadet . . . ?"

"Bowen," Pierce said.

"So he's the one?" Rhane asked as he glanced over at Agent O'Keefe.

"That's him, all right."

"Go on," Rhane said, turning his attention back to Pierce.

"If you really did come from Gathmara," Pierce said, "how do we know that you didn't kill the real Agent Rhane, shape-shift to look just like him, and infiltrate our campus?"

"You don't, so I suggest you sleep lightly tonight," Agent Rhane said with a smile that made the hair on the back of Colt's neck stand on end. "And for the record, I'm not here to make friends. I'm here to teach you how to survive on Gathmara so you have a snowball's chance of accomplishing your mission."

CHAPTER 11

W hat do you say we start with Goliath?" Agent Rhane said. O'Keefe nodded and entered a series of commands in his handheld device. The air shimmered, and moments later a thirty-foot robot appeared in the middle of the floor, its head nearly touching the top of the domed ceiling. Covered in thick iron plating that looked like scraps from old tanks, it had gun turrets on its shoulders, cannons welded to its forearms, and rocket boosters embedded in its heels.

"Now Goliath here is a Tracker, which for all intents and purposes is a walking tank with limited artificial intelligence," Rhane said. "Any idea how you take one down?"

"Nukes," Ethan said.

"Fair enough, but what about civilians within the blast radius?"

"Hit the knee joints with rocket-propelled grenades," Colt said.

"Now we're talking," Rhane said. "You the squad leader, then?"

"Yes, sir," Colt said.

Rhane stared at him with narrowed eyes, and again Colt felt the telltale hair on the back of his neck stand on end once more. "Then you're the one . . . the Betrayer?"

Colt tried to hold Rhane's gaze, but it was so intense that he had to look away.

"That 'aw shucks' humility won't get you far, cadet. Not on the other side of the portal. Once you enter the jungles of Gathmara, you can bet that just about everything that moves will be looking to kill you—and I'm not just talking about the Thule. Understand?"

"Yes, sir."

"Then what do you say we visit Dresh and see if we can't survive long enough to reach the facility where they're storing the engine that will open the gateway?"

O'Keefe activated the hologram chamber, and the sterile room became a lush jungle where vines covered in bright red and yellow blooms coiled around trees that rose high overhead. Pools of stagnant water dotted the ground, and even though it was an artificial environment, the air was suddenly hot and humid.

"Believe it or not, this halogram used to be a suburb not far from the capital," Rhane said. "Koenig found out that someone had been harboring the son of a rival warlord, so he destroyed the entire town—women, children, and all."

Colt started to notice the broken remains of buildings that were buried under the vines. Trees grew from the windows, and crumbled streets were overrun by vegetation that sprouted from the cracks. There were rusted vehicles, including what looked like a military transport with eight wheels and something that looked like a car with wings, which Rhane explained was a hovercraft.

He led them through the jungle, pointing out a variety of plant life. Some were edible. Some poisonous. All were stunningly beautiful. "Whatever you do, don't drink any water that you haven't put through your purifier," he explained. "The parasites will eat through the wall of your stomach and you'll bleed to death."

"Lovely," Danielle said as she sidestepped a puddle.

Eventually they came to the outskirts of a massive city that rose before them like a forest of concrete and glass. "Welcome to Dresh, the city of wonder," Rhane said with a healthy dose of sarcasm. "In case you weren't yet convinced that Koenig is a monster, he wiped out half the population with a strain of virus that was created inside the halls of Trident Biotech."

"Why?" Pierce asked.

"To scare the other warlords," Rhane said. "After all, if he was willing to kill his own people, what would he do to those who opposed him?"

Agent O'Keefe called up a transport vehicle that materialized on the street not far from where they were standing. They all piled in, and Rhane drove them through abandoned city streets lined with propaganda posters that were weathered and torn, each showing Koenig in his human form.

"That's it," he said, pointing to a massive domed structure on the horizon. "The reactor core that will power the gateway is inside those walls. Now all you have to do is find a way to get inside and blow it up. But let's save that adventure for another day. I'm thinking we should start with something easy . . . Agent O'Keefe?"

"Yes, Agent Rhane?" O'Keefe's voice replied through a loudspeaker.

"You still have Goliath cued up?"

"That I do."

"What would you say to activating him? I wonder if our young cadets could survive for at least ten minutes."

"There's only one way to find out," O'Keefe said, and suddenly Goliath loomed before them in the street.

It was all over quickly. Phantom Squad didn't last to the five-minute mark, and Agent O'Keefe gave them all a failing grade.

"Like it matters," Pierce grumbled.

"What do you mean by that, Cadet Pierce Bowen?" Glyph asked.

"We can't beat the Thule no matter what we do."

‖‖‖‖‖‖‖‖‖‖‖‖‖‖‖‖‖‖‖‖‖‖‖‖‖

The words haunted Colt for the rest of the day.

Pierce wasn't the first person to think that things were hopeless, and he wasn't going to be the last. People were flocking to remote locations by the tens of thousands. It was impossible for grocery stores to keep canned goods and bottled water on the shelves. Churches, synagogues, and mosques were filled to capacity around the clock. A few days earlier Colt and the other squad leaders had even been briefed about a group that was starting to worship the Thule in hopes that they would be shown mercy once Earth was conquered.

But this was different. Pierce was brash. Arrogant. Over-bearing. He had never—not once—shown any kind of weakness or vulnerability. So why now? Had his dad told him that the next attack was going to happen any day? Did he find out the president was actually a shape-shifting Thule? Or was he just mentally and emotionally exhausted, like everyone else?

Colt looked up at the clock tower. It wasn't quite three in the afternoon, which meant he had an hour before he was to report to the training facility for more hand-to-hand combat lessons with Lieutenant Lohr, the Tharik from a wooded planet called Nemus who looked like Bigfoot fused with a robot. Instead of going back to his dorm, he found an empty study room in the library that had a warm fire blazing in the hearth.

The tension left his body as he sat in an overstuffed leather chair and kicked his boots up onto the coffee table. Between the warm air and soft throw pillows, it didn't take long for his eyes to grow heavy. He blinked once and then twice, fighting to stay awake, but his head fell against his shoulder and he could feel the drool sliding down the corner of his mouth.

"Colt?"

Startled, he sat up, and for a moment he wasn't sure where he was. He shook his head and turned around, and saw Miranda Patel standing beside the fireplace.

"I thought that was you," she said. "What are you doing here? Aren't you supposed to be training for your new job?"

Colt swiped the drool from his chin and forced a smile. "Oh . . . um, yeah," he said, trying to kick-start his brain so he could form a clear thought. "I, ah . . . well, we had practice this morning." He tried to stand up but slipped on his backpack and fell back into his chair. "You're talking about the Phantom Flyer thing, right?"

"Are you okay?"

"Yeah, fine," he said, kicking his backpack out of the way so he could stand without making a fool of himself. "So what have you been up to?" He leaned against the chair, then stood up straight when he realized how lame he must look.

"I got stood up for lunch the other day," Miranda said.

"Really? By who?"

"You."

"Wait, you were serious?" Colt said, still finding it hard to believe that Miranda Patel actually wanted to have lunch with him.

"Of course. What about—"

"Attention, all cadets," a synthesized voice said through the speakers in the ceiling. "Jackal, Blizzard, Lightning, Phantom, and Anvil Squadrons need to report to Helipad Delta immediately. I repeat, Jackal, Blizzard, Lightning, Phantom, and Anvil Squadrons, please report to Helipad Delta. This is not a drill."

"Phantom," Colt said. "That's me. I've got to go."

Miranda's eyes went wide and her dark skin grew pale. "Do you think we're under attack?" she asked as a group of cadets ran past the study room, their boots echoing down through the hall.

"I doubt it; they would have made all the squads report."

"Then what is it?"

Colt shrugged. "I guess I'm about to find out." He started to walk past her, but she placed her hand against his chest.

When he looked down, their faces were mere inches apart. He was intoxicated by the scent of her hair. Her skin. Her breath.

It felt warm against his neck, and he just stood there, unable to move as he looked into her eyes.

He swallowed. It felt like ten thousand fireflies were alight in his stomach at the same time, their tiny wings beating. Tickling. He wondered if he was going to faint.

She leaned closer, lips slightly parted. Her hand reached up and flames lit where her fingers caressed his cheek. She reached behind his head and drew him close. He thought about Lily and started to resist, but he was short of breath. As her lips touched his, there was an explosion of sensation.

"Come back," she said, the words little more than a whisper in his ear.

He nodded, unable to form a coherent thought, much less a complete sentence.

:: CHAPTER 12 ::

Two dozen cadets were already gathered at the helipad by the time Colt got there. Some were crying. Others looked angry. Most just stood there with blank stares.

He looked around to see if anyone else from Phantom Squad was there and spotted Danielle standing next to Jonas, who was patting her shoulder and speaking to her in hushed tones.

"What happened?" Colt asked.

Danielle turned and looked at him with tears in her eyes. For a moment he thought she was going to say something, but she just shook her head and buried her face in her hands.

"There was another attack," Jonas said.

"What?"

"A portal opened up over Philadelphia about an hour ago, and it was big enough to let a Class 4 Hydra through—you know, one of the Thule carriers. Anyway, they aren't sure how many are dead, but it looks worse than Rose Hill."

"That was ten thousand people."

"I know," Jonas said. "They think this might be double."

Colt felt as though someone had hit him in the chest with a sledgehammer. Twenty thousand people. And if they didn't do something soon, it was only going to get worse. "Are they sending us to Philly?" he asked.

"We're still waiting for orders," Jonas said.

No longer able to hold back, Danielle sobbed openly. Tears streaked her face, and her shoulders shook. Colt placed his arms around her, and she leaned against him. He stroked her hair but offered no words of encouragement. Telling her that everything was going to be all right would only be an empty promise.

More cadets joined them, and soon squads started to form, each distinguishable by its accent color. Jackal had orange insignias on their shoulder pads, chest plates, and helmets. Blizzard was light blue. Lightning was yellow. Anvil was purple. And Phantom was gray.

Besides Colt, Danielle, Stacy, Grey, and Glyph, the other members of Phantom Squad were Pierce, the arrogant blowhard, and Ethan Foley, Grey and Colt's other roommate, and Jonas. Oz had been part of Phantom Squad before he was expelled, but Superintendent Thorne didn't replace him. Even though it meant they were short one man, Colt took it as a hopeful sign. Maybe one day she'd let him back.

Most of the cadets milled about the helipad chatting nervously as they waited for orders, but Jackal Squad stood at attention on the periphery as Gulrukh Mirza, their squad leader, inspected their weapons. Colt thought about doing the same, but he was missing a member.

"Anyone see Pierce?"

"There he is," Ethan said, pointing back toward campus. "Over there with the dog."

"I don't think that's a dog."

"Agreed, Squad Leader Colt McAlister," Glyph said.

The creature on the other end of the leash looked more like a wolf than a dog, but its chest was too wide, its snout too short, and its coat was moss green. It loped toward them next to Pierce, taking long strides as it lowered its head to sniff the ground.

"What is that thing?" Jonas asked, taking a step back as the creature sniffed at his feet.

"A genetically altered Malinois." Pierce smiled as though he was enjoying Jonas's discomfort. "Her official name is Prototype A-F-6, but I call her Fang."

"What's she doing here?" Colt asked.

"She's part of the Senate Intelligence Committee's Alien Extermination Initiative. She tracks 'em, we kill 'em."

"Most aliens do not require tracking or killing, Cadet Pierce Bowen," Glyph said.

"Whatever. You know what I meant."

"That doesn't make it any less offensive. Besides, the vomeronasal organ in the roof of my mouth makes me eminently more qualified to track scents than the primitive canines on this planet—including your prototype."

"Get off me!" Jonas shouted. Fang was standing on her hind legs and licking his face.

"Heel!" Pierce yanked on the dog's collar and she walked over to stand next to him, but her eyes were locked on Jonas.

"She's a beauty," said a voice behind them.

They all turned to see a creature that looked like it was part Bigfoot and part robot walking toward them. At well over seven feet tall, its massive body was covered in fur the color of rust. It had broad shoulders, muscles like iron cables, and a second head made out of metal and bolted over its left shoulder. If that wasn't strange enough, its left arm and right leg had been replaced by mechanical prosthetics, making it look like some kind of freak experiment gone bad.

"Thank you, Lieutenant," Pierce said.

"Let's hope she's as good in the field as she was in those tests."

"She will be, sir. Guaranteed."

Lieutenant Lohr smiled, revealing a wicked set of incisors as his second robotic head turned to stare at the dog. The cadets went quiet. "All right," he said. "By now most of you have heard that there was a second attack just outside of Philadelphia. Before you start asking questions, I'll tell you what I know.

"At least one Hydra slipped through the portal, and there are conflicting reports that one and possibly two transports made it through as well. That means we have up to one thousand unwelcome guests causing havoc up and down the Eastern Seaboard.

"Local authorities did their best," he continued, "but those six-armed lizards made it all the way to New Brunswick before soldiers from the 10th Mountain Division engaged them. They've managed to slow them down, but the fighting is still hot and heavy. Reinforcements are on their way from as far away as Fort Bragg and Shaw Air Force Base, but things are a little dicey at the moment."

"Are we going to New Brunswick?" a cadet from Anvil Squad asked. He was strong, with black hair and matching eyes.

"Next time you interrupt me, Cadet Johnson, you'll be on skid patrol."

"Skid patrol, sir?"

"It means you'll be scrubbing tighty whiteys by hand until your fingernails start to bleed. Is that understood?"

"Yes, sir."

"Jarrod Johnson on skid patrol? That would be hilarious," Ethan said.

"You looking to join him?" Lieutenant Lohr asked.

Ethan gulped. "No, sir."

"That's what I thought." Lohr turned back to the rest of the crowd, but his robotic head kept staring at Ethan. "Now, thanks to the stupidity of youth and those fancy battle suits, most of you think you're invincible. But don't fool yourselves. War is hell. Do you hear me? I can promise that the second one of those lizards comes charging at you, you're going to want to ball up in a fetal position and call for your mamas, but there's only one problem. Your mamas won't be there to protect you. Understood?"

"Yes, sir," a few of the cadets said in chorus.

"Again!"

"Yes, sir!" they all shouted.

"Better," Lieutenant Lohr said. "Since most active duty military east of the Mississippi are on the front lines trying to stop those lizards from reaching New York City, we've been asked to pick up the slack. I need each squad leader front and center. The rest of you, sit tight. Your rides will be here any minute."

:: CHAPTER 13 ::

A Boeing CH-47 Chinook helicopter took Phantom Squad to Beaver Valley Nuclear Power Plant outside of Shippingport, Pennsylvania, where an engineer claimed he'd seen strange shapes emerge from the river near the plant. He said that one of them even scaled the Shippingport Bridge like a giant spider.

"That's just about far enough," a man wearing what looked like riot gear said. He was short and plump and had a thick mustache that had grown over his lip, and even though he wasn't very intimidating, he was holding an assault rifle with a grenade launcher mounted under the barrel. So were the two men who stood behind him.

"We're with the Department of Alien Affairs," Colt said, slowly raising his hands to show that he wasn't a threat.

"Then what are you doing with that thing?" The man nodded at Glyph, whose eyes grew wide with fear.

"He's with us."

"I don't think so," the man said.

Colt narrowed his eyes. "Cadet Gundar is a cadet at the Intergalactic Defense Academy and is here under orders from the director of the Department of Alien Affairs. We're here to check on a disturbance, but if you prefer we can turn around and leave."

The man started chewing the inside of his lip as though contemplating what to do next. "How do we know he ain't one of them?"

"Because he's a Fimorian," Colt said. "See? He has two arms, not six."

"That's true enough, I suppose," the man said, lowering his rifle. "The name's Damewood. Chadwick Damewood. I'm the head of security at this facility."

"I'm Cadet McAlister, and this—"

"McAlister, you say?" Damewood interrupted. "Now where have I heard that name before?" He stroked his mustache as he cocked his head to the side. "Hey, wait. You're that kid—the Phantom Flyer's grandson, right?"

Colt rolled his eyes, which were hidden behind his helmet. "Yes, sir."

"Ain't you supposed to be traveling around with that air show and whatnot?"

"Right now I'm focused on helping you secure this facility," Colt said.

"No offense, but it might be best if your alien friend there waited outside," Damewood said. "The employees . . . well, let's just say I don't think they'll take kindly to his ilk, if you catch my meaning."

"No, I don't," Colt said.

"Don't say I didn't warn you."

After the meeting they broke into teams. Colt led Alpha Team—Danielle, Glyph, and Jonas—through a sweep of the facilities, while Stacy led Bravo—Pierce and his dog, Grey, and Ethan—down to the riverbank.

The facility was massive, with cement walls, miles of pipes, and far too many nooks and crannies where Thule could hide. Glyph spent most of the time hunched over as he ducked through doorways and patrolled halls that weren't built for someone his height.

Everyone in the plant was on edge, and it didn't take long to discover that the employees were upset that management had let an alien onto the premises.

"What's that thing doing here?" one asked.

"Since when do humans mix with their kind?" another said.

Glyph acted like he couldn't hear them, but Colt was growing frustrated.

"We should round 'em all up and kill 'em before they turn on us," said a short man with a thick mat of orange hair.

"What did you say?" Colt demanded.

The color drained from the man's face as Colt stepped toward him.

"I asked you a question."

"Don't." Danielle placed her hand on Colt's shoulder, but he pulled away.

"His words are protected by the First Amendment, Squad Leader Colt McAlister," Glyph said as he placed his hand on Colt's shoulder. "And in truth, I cannot fault him for being afraid. We all are."

Colt glared at the worker, who stood there with his back against the wall. "Go on," he said, and the man practically ran down the hall before he disappeared around a corner.

"Thank you for standing up for me," Glyph said. "But it truly wasn't necessary."

"Yes. It was," Colt said.

"Wait a minute," Danielle said. "Have either of you seen Jonas?"

CHAPTER 14

They searched the facility for nearly an hour before a security guard said that one of the cameras had caught Jonas leaving the facility and heading for the riverbank.

His tracks were easy enough to follow. They led across the lawn and down a path to the river, but they stopped at the water.

"Can you pick up his scent?" Colt asked, turning to Glyph, who just shook his head.

"He wasn't wearing a jet pack," Danielle said. "And if he tried to swim to the other side, he would have died from hypothermia."

"I don't see any signs of struggle," Glyph said.

"So he just disappeared?" Colt asked, frustrated as he tried to make sense of what had happened.

"Bravo Leader, this is Alpha Leader, over," Colt said into his comlink.

"This is Bravo Leader," Stacy replied.

"Any luck?"

"Not unless you count losing Pierce's stupid dog," she said. "He let it off its leash, and it bolted."

"Please tell me that was a joke."

"Sorry."

Colt sighed. "We'll look for Jonas, you find the dog, and we'll meet back at the entrance at 0930."

"Roger that," Stacy said.

"We need to find that dog before it wanders into somebody's backyard," Colt said as he turned back to Glyph and Danielle.

"What about Jonas?" Danielle asked.

"I'll circle back and see if I can find a different set of tracks," Colt said. "You two help them find the dog."

॥॥॥॥॥॥॥॥॥॥॥॥॥॥॥॥॥॥॥॥॥॥

Colt pulled a small disc from a pouch on his belt. The moment he hit the button, a three-dimensional holographic map of the area projected into the air.

"Where are you hiding?" he murmured as he walked back up to the lawn in front of the nuclear power plant. But there were no other tracks, so he ended up back at the riverbank.

Overhead a smattering of stars dotted the sky as the moon fought to break out from behind a bank of clouds, and a cold breeze whipped across the water. Colt picked up a smooth stone and was ready to skim it across the surface of the water when the hair on the back of his neck stood on end.

Something had moved up ahead.

He doused the lights mounted on his helmet and switched the pattern of his Whitlock Armor System to nighttime camouflage.

Odds were that it was Jonas, but why would seeing Jonas trigger Colt's internal early warning system? Something wasn't right.

Colt crept along the riverbank, thankful that the rush of the water masked most of the sound as he attempted to channel his inner spy. The telescopic night vision goggles helped and so did his enhanced vision from his Thule DNA, which is why he saw Jonas standing next to a man on an unmarked armored ultralight before either of them spotted him.

"What are you up to, Jonas?" Colt whispered aloud as he watched the man hand Jonas an envelope.

Jonas looked around before he removed his pack and placed the envelope inside. A moment later the man on the ultralight took off, and Jonas scrambled up the embankment back toward the nuclear power plant.

Colt waited until he thought Jonas was far enough away that he wouldn't be able to hear or see him approach, and then he crept along the shore and followed him through the thick brush and up the hill.

Something moved.

"Jonas?" Colt asked.

No response.

"Is that you?"

A massive shape burst from the thicket and grabbed Colt by the forearm with its jaw. It was Pierce's genetically altered Malinois, but why was it attacking? The armor held, but the pressure was excruciating as the dog swung its head back and forth like it wanted to rip Colt's arm out of its socket.

Something popped in his shoulder, and the searing pain sent Colt to his knees.

Adrenaline surged, and the pain gave way to a feeling of euphoria. Colt felt powerful. Unstoppable. He grabbed the dog by the nape of its neck and yanked it from his arm. Its jaws snapped as it fought to gain another hold, but Colt stood up and threw the animal against a boulder.

There was a loud crack, and it fell in a heap. It started to bubble and bones began to crack. Fur gave way to scales, two extra sets of arms grew from its back, and its paws turned to fingers.

"You can shape-shift into animals?" Colt asked.

The Thule that had been a dog just moments before stood and took a step toward him but staggered. It took a second step and fell to one knee, bellowing in pain. Its chest heaved as it struggled to breathe, but then it shifted once more.

A chill crawled up Colt's spine. "Who are you?" he asked as he stood there looking at a perfect copy of himself.

"Who are you?" the shapeshifter mimicked, its voice matching his in pitch and inflection.

"Colt!"

He spun around to see Danielle and Glyph, who were standing on a ridge at the top of the embankment.

"We heard something and—" Her voice broke off. "Which one is you?"

"I am," the two Colts said together.

She raised her sniper rifle.

"Dani, it's me," Colt said, unable to tell which Colt she was aiming at.

"He's lying," the doppelgänger said.

"Please, Dani," Colt said. "You don't want to do this."

"What's my dog's name?" she asked.

"Wolfgang."

Danielle pulled the trigger, and the doppelgänger fell to its knees before its face hit the ground.

:: CHAPTER 15 ::

When Pierce learned that Danielle had shot his dog, he was furious, until Colt pointed out that it was a shape-shifting Thule and that somehow it had come from a program funded by the senate committee that Pierce's own father sat on.

"As for you," Colt said, turning to Jonas, "start talking."

Jonas didn't say a word. He just stared at the USB drive that Colt held between his fingers.

"He's probably a shapeshifter too," Pierce said. "You need to put him in restraints or shoot him with a tranquilizer or—"

"Enough," Colt said, and for once Pierce stopped talking.

"It's not what you think," Jonas finally said.

"Okay, then what is it?"

"If I tell you, they won't help me anymore."

"If you don't, you're going to end up in one of those underground prisons," Colt said. "The choice is yours."

Jonas sighed. "Have any of you heard of the Tesla Society?" None of them had.

"What about you?" Jonas asked, looking directly at Colt. "Has your grandfather ever mentioned it?"

"Not that I remember."

"It's kind of like the Illuminati, only most of the members are scientists and inventors. You know, people like Einstein and Steve Jobs. Anyway, the government wrote them a blank check and asked them to find a way to predict where the Thule are going to open the gateway, and then shut it down."

"What does that have to do with the guy on the armored ultralight?" Colt asked.

Jonas closed his eyes and took a deep breath, as though what he was about to say was going to be painful. "I know one of the members. He has a theory that he can't prove, so he asked me to help."

"You?" Pierce asked. "Yeah, right."

"Leave him alone," Stacy said.

"My contact can't send the data over e-mail, so he has it delivered," Jonas said. "And since the information is . . . well, sensitive, he prefers to deliver it whenever we're on patrol. That way it doesn't go through inspection at the front desk."

"What kind of data?" Colt asked.

"The coordinates for every active portal since we started tracking them back in 1956."

:: CHAPTER 16 ::

Phantom Squad didn't get back to campus until after ten the next night, and Colt rolled his eyes when he saw the *Phantasmic . . . March to Victory* posters already hanging on one of the kiosks.

He offered to walk Stacy back to her dorm under the auspices that he didn't trust Pierce, which was partially true.

"Can I ask you something?" he said as his boots crunched on the freshly fallen snow.

"Sure."

"You and Pierce . . . you weren't actually . . . well, you know . . ."

"What, dating?" Stacy laughed, breaking the tension. "I don't know what you would call it, but we were close—at least for a while."

"Sorry, it's none of my business." Colt turned his attention to a squirrel that scampered up a tree. He hoped she didn't notice he was blushing.

"It's fine," Stacy said. "There's a reason I didn't tell anyone that we knew each other back home. Most people think he's an arrogant, spoiled-rotten jerk."

"No comment."

Stacy smiled. "He wasn't always like that. I mean, yeah, I suppose you could say he was always . . . well, confident."

"Confident?"

"Things just come easy for him. I'd study for hours and end up with a B on a chemistry test, and he'd blow it off and end up with an A. It was infuriating, but I'm pretty sure he has a photographic memory. It was the same with sports—he was the star on our basketball team even though he never took it seriously. But everything changed when he found out his dad cheated on his mom. He got angry."

"Is that when you guys broke up?"

"Something like that. There's a part of me that still likes him, as strange as that may sound. It's just that I know how much it hurts when your parents get divorced, so I guess that's why I'm not as hard on him as I should be."

"I'm sorry," Colt said. "I had no idea."

"You don't have anything to be sorry about. You're not the one who had an affair with one of my teachers."

Colt stopped, his jaw hanging open. "Wait, are you serious?"

Stacy nodded. "Crazy, isn't it? I was so embarrassed that if I hadn't gotten the invitation from CHAOS, I would have emptied my savings account and moved to a remote jungle in South America."

"I don't even know what to say."

"Danielle was right—you're not so bad," Stacy said with a grin.

"Don't believe everything you hear."

"What if I told you that she sneaked out the other night to go and see Oz?"

"Now you're just messing with me."

Stacy raised a single eyebrow. "Are you sure?"

Colt couldn't imagine Danielle breaking the rules like that, especially after everything that happened with Oz and his dad. Then again, it was only a matter of time before they admitted to the rest of the world that they were more than friends.

"She's liked him for a long time," Stacy said as she cut across the lawn toward a bridge that led to the girls' dormitories.

"Yeah, I kind of figured."

"All right, now it's time for me to ask you a question."

Colt knew he was in trouble from the way Stacy was smiling.

"Tell me about Lily," she said.

"What about her?" Colt said, trying to sound nonchalant.

"Do you miss her?"

He bit his lower lip and made a silent vow to get even with Danielle. What was he supposed to say? That he thought about Lily all the time, or that it didn't matter because he was pretty sure she had moved on?

"You do, don't you?" Stacy's smile was gone.

"I don't know," Colt said. "I guess. But it's not like she was my girlfriend or anything."

"If you say so."

"I'm serious," Colt said, sounding angrier than he had

intended. He lowered his voice and continued. "After my parents died, Lily was . . . I don't know, I guess she was there for me. Her birth parents died when she was little, so she knew what I was going through. It's kind of like you and Pierce, I guess."

"It didn't hurt that she's beautiful."

Colt frowned.

"Danielle showed me a picture."

"She is pretty." Colt shrugged, trying to keep his emotions in check. Talking about Lily made him miss her more than ever, and yet he liked spending time with Stacy. Then again, what did it matter, if the world was about to end?

"You don't have to be embarrassed," Stacy said as they approached the front porch.

"Yeah, well, I better get going," Colt said. "Don't want to get caught out after curfew."

"Like it matters," Stacy said. "What are they going to do, expel you? Everyone knows that you're our only hope against the Thule. I'm pretty sure you could do whatever you want and they wouldn't touch you."

"I doubt it."

Stacy leaned over and kissed him on the cheek. "Thanks for walking me home," she said.

She ran up the front steps and through the door, leaving Colt more confused about his feelings than ever. Lily seemed so far away, and Stacy was real. Then there was Miranda . . . not that he had feelings for her. Not really, anyway. Still, even if she only liked him because she thought he was going to be famous, it felt good.

"Colt!"

He turned around and saw Grey and Ethan running toward him.

"We've been looking all over for you," Ethan said.

"Yeah, everywhere," Grey added. "Have you heard?"

"Heard what?" Colt asked, more than a little annoyed. He wondered how long they had been watching him.

"The Black Sun Militia broke their treaty with Koenig's Defense Corps, and there's a rumor that the Vril will be next," Ethan said. "You know what that means, right? They're going to be so caught up fighting each other that they won't be able to invade Earth."

"We'll see," Colt said.

"Oh yeah," Ethan said as he handed him a piece of paper. "I almost forgot. Have you seen these?"

Colt turned it over, and when he saw a *Phantasmic . . . March to Victory* poster he crumpled it up.

"What are you doing?" Grey said. "That thing is awesome."

"Yeah, I was going to have you sign it so I could send it back home to my brother," Ethan said.

Colt took a deep breath and exhaled slowly. "Maybe later, all right? I just need to clear my head."

CHAPTER 17

G rey and Ethan were still asleep when Colt slipped out of bed the next morning. He hesitated a moment, looking at Oz's empty bunk as he wondered if Danielle had been sneaking out at night to meet him. The thought of them dating, much less kissing, made him uncomfortable. It wasn't that he was jealous. He just thought of Danielle as his kid sister, and he didn't want *anyone* kissing her—and that included his best friend.

A flashing light caught his eye, and he walked over to his dresser to find that he had a message waiting for him on his tablet. It was an e-mail from Danielle, who wanted to meet him at his grandpa's apartment after breakfast. Apparently she and Jonas had spent the entire night and into the morning poring over the data from the Tesla Society, and they'd had a breakthrough.

"I better not be late for my training scenario with Agent Rhane," Colt grumbled under his breath. As much as he wanted to believe that the Black Sun Militia breaking their treaty would keep the Thule from invading, he still wanted to be ready.

Colt took a quick shower, changed into his uniform, and stopped by the commissary to grab a protein bar and an energy drink. By the time he got to the apartment, Danielle was sitting at the kitchen table with a plate of scrambled eggs, toast, and bacon and a tall glass of orange juice.

Grandpa had an open invitation to join the faculty at the Intergalactic Defense Academy, but he had no intention of accepting the offer. He claimed the only reason he was still living in campus housing was because he wanted to make sure there was a smooth transition with the new leadership team—but Colt had a feeling that he was sticking around to make sure nobody else tried to assassinate his grandson.

"Where's my breakfast?" he asked.

"There's the fridge, help yourself," Grandpa said as Danielle stifled a laugh.

"I knew he liked you better than me," Colt said as he stole a strip of bacon.

"Was there ever any doubt?" Grandpa was approaching his eighty-sixth birthday, but if it weren't for the gray hair he wouldn't look a day over fifty. He was tall and thin with perfect posture, wide shoulders, and a narrow waist that made him look every bit the superhero he truly was.

The doorbell rang.

"I bet that's Jonas," Danielle said, wiping her mouth with a napkin as she got up and followed Grandpa to the door.

Jonas looked nervous. He kept looking over his shoulder, and the moment Grandpa invited him inside he slammed the door shut and locked the dead bolt. Next he closed all the blinds and poked his head into the pantry, checking behind the door before he sat down at the table and chugged down the rest of Danielle's orange juice.

"Is someone following you?" Grandpa asked.

"To tell you the truth, Colonel McAlister, I'm not sure," Jonas said.

"Call me Murdoch," Grandpa said.

"Yes, sir, thank you."

Grandpa poured him another glass of orange juice. "So is someone going to tell me what kind of trouble the three of you have gotten yourselves into, or is this simply a social call?"

"We discovered something important about the Thule," Danielle said. "I mean, right now it's just a theory—but it's a sound theory. And if we're right, it could change everything!"

"Slow down," Grandpa said.

Danielle took a deep breath and explained how she and Jonas were convinced that there was a direct correlation between portals and what they were calling "randoms," and how those randoms might lead to the Thule gateway.

"Randoms, is it? How do they work?" Grandpa asked.

"We're not exactly sure," Danielle said. "I mean, they're not portals or even tears in the space-time fabric. They aren't soft spots either."

"In truth, they don't even qualify as precursors," Jonas added. "They're like tiny pinholes that come and go, but more are showing up every day."

"And you think there's a pattern?" Grandpa said. "Some kind of hidden message?"

"Yes, sir."

Grandpa took a sip of coffee, but his eyes never left Jonas. "I think there may be more to the story."

"Like what?" Danielle asked.

"That data had to come from somewhere, and I'm guessing you either stole it or you have an inside source. Either way, it explains why Cadet Hickman is so fidgety."

"We didn't steal it—at least not directly," Jonas said. "But the thing is . . . well . . . we can't tell you where it came from."

Grandpa took another sip of his coffee. "How long before you find the gateway?"

"That's the problem," Jonas said. "It could be this afternoon or a year from now. We just don't know."

"One week," Grandpa said.

"For what?" Danielle asked.

"That's when you present your findings."

"But—"

Grandpa held up his hand to cut Jonas off. "You're not getting a second more, so I suggest you get up from that chair, walk out the door, and get to work."

"Yes, sir."

"As for you," Grandpa said to Colt. "You have somewhere else you have to be."

:: CHAPTER 18 ::

Koenig wants to see me?" Colt asked as he and his grandfather followed a pair of DAA agents down a path that
led to a bank of trees lining the Potomac River. Aldrich
Koenig was the former president of Trident Biotech. He was not
only responsible for the murder of Colt's parents but was also
supposed to be the leader of the largest Thule army on Gathmara.

"He said that he'll provide certain information if you'll talk
to him, but he won't say what it's about."

"Where is he?"

"In a prison beneath the tunnels."

"Here? On campus?" Colt couldn't believe what he was
hearing. "You're telling me the mastermind behind this entire
invasion has been locked up here since he was arrested back in
October?"

"That about sums it up."

"Why didn't you tell me?"

"You never asked."

"Is it about what happened with the Black Sun Militia?"

"Hard to say," Grandpa replied. "But we'll know soon enough."

The academy grounds used to belong to a private university founded by Thomas Jefferson. The president of the university was an abolitionist who constructed a series of tunnels to help fugitive slaves escape to the North. Colt found the tunnels when he accidentally fell through a shaft. Since then he had been down in the tunnels on more than one occasion—including the night that Heinrich Krone, the Thule assassin Oz's dad had hired, was killed. And Colt didn't remember seeing a prison anywhere down there.

"Is that why they attacked?" Colt asked. "Were they looking for Koenig?"

"It's hard to tell, but if they were, they didn't find him."

They followed the DAA agents down a trail that led to a small cabin that had a sagging roof and broken windows. One of the agents reached for a rusted mailbox that hid a biometric scanner. He placed his hand against the glass; green circles flashed around his fingers and thumb, and the door opened.

"In you go," Grandpa said.

Colt stepped into an elevator car without buttons, and a moment later they started their descent. "How far down are we going?" he asked.

"Far enough," Grandpa said.

The elevator stopped, and the doors opened to a long corridor where the walls were metal instead of dirt. Grandpa stepped out and Colt followed, but the DAA agents didn't move.

"This shouldn't take long," Grandpa said.

As the doors to the elevator closed, Colt couldn't help but feel trapped. Sure, there were agents from Whitlock Armor Systems stationed every ten feet, but for all Colt knew they were Thule in disguise. For that matter, Grandpa could have been a Thule too. It smelled like a trap.

"You're a bit jittery," Grandpa said as he led Colt through a series of checkpoints where the DAA agents simply saluted and let them pass.

"I'm fine," Colt said, even though the hair on the back of his neck was standing on end. But if he admitted his suspicion, and it really was Grandpa, he was going to look like he was losing his mind. And if the man with him was one of the Thule, then Colt would lose the element of surprise. Either way, he figured it was best to keep quiet.

There were no pictures on the walls, the doors were evenly spaced, and thanks to their armor and helmets, all the agents looked exactly alike, give or take a few inches, all of which meant that it was easy to get turned around.

"This place is a maze," Colt said. "How do you know where you're going?"

"I've been down here a time or two over the last few weeks," Grandpa said as he took long strides. "You start to pick up on the patterns, but it's confusing on purpose. Makes an escape—or a rescue, for that matter—that much harder."

"No kidding."

They turned down what looked to be a dead end, where two guards stood on either side of an average door.

"What's his mood like today?" Grandpa asked.

The nearest guard shrugged. "Same as always, I guess," he said as a panel in the wall opened up. A metal sphere flew out and hovered next to Grandpa, who didn't seem to notice. "Sorry, sir," the guard said. "You know the routine."

"No need to apologize, you're just doing your job." Grandpa watched as an arm with a needle on the end extended from the sphere. He held out his hand, and it slammed into his index finger like a woodpecker taking to its favorite tree. A red dot of blood formed on Grandpa's fingertip as a second arm unfurled, this one holding some kind of swab. It dabbed at the blood and held the swab under its belly where a door opened up, revealing a green light.

"What's it doing?" Colt asked, backing up until he hit the wall.

"It's just a blood test," Grandpa said as the orb extended a third arm.

"Would you care for a bandage?" it asked with a polite, if synthesized, voice.

"That won't be necessary," Grandpa said.

"Very well," the orb said. "One moment, please, while I complete the analysis."

"Take your time."

Colt started to calculate what he would do if Grandpa weren't actually Grandpa. He figured that he could get one good shot—probably to the throat—before he took off down the hall, but the only way it was going to work was if the DAA agents weren't part of the ruse. He'd need them to tie fake-Grandpa up, or there was no way he was going to make it back to the elevators without a fight. But if the agents were Thule too . . .

"Thank you, Colonel. You are free to visit the prisoner," the orb said, interrupting Colt's thoughts.

"Your turn," Grandpa said. "Go ahead; it doesn't hurt any more than a bee sting."

"Yeah, all right," Colt said, wondering if the needle was strong enough to pierce his skin. He swallowed hard as he raised a nervous hand. As the orb scuttled over and raised its arm to strike, Colt closed his eyes.

"That wasn't so bad, was it?"

Colt hadn't felt a thing, and as he opened his eyes he saw Grandpa standing there with his arms folded across his chest.

"How . . . ?" he asked.

"The needle?" Grandpa said. "Thule tech from Trident Biotech."

"Interesting," the orb said, as though a machine could be surprised by the results. "I'm detecting an alien contaminate."

:: CHAPTER 19 ::

Colt watched from the corner of his eye as one of the guards slid his finger over the trigger of an assault rifle. His chest constricted, his mouth was dry, and swallowing suddenly became difficult. *Relax*, he thought as he tried to control his breathing. *Everything is going to be fine.*

"Check the numbers against your database," Grandpa said, his voice steady. "Or if you need to, put a call in to Doc Roth and he'll set you straight."

"That won't be necessary," the orb said. "The alien contaminates are spawning at an increased rate but are still within an acceptable range. Verification is positive. Thank you for your patience, Cadet McAlister." Without another word, the orb's arms contracted and it flew back into the compartment, where the panel slid shut.

"Breathe," Grandpa said with a wink.

Colt exhaled as the DAA agent took his finger off the trigger and opened the door. The room looked like a giant pit where a glass cage stood on a pillar that was at least twenty feet around and forty feet tall. The only way across the chasm that separated them from the cage was a narrow bridge without any rails.

"You have visitors," one of the guards announced through a sound system.

Aldrich Koenig looked up and smiled as he removed his reading glasses. His teeth were perfect, and so were his blond hair, square jaw, broad shoulders, and narrow waist. The blue of his eyes matched the color of his tie, and his shoes were polished to the point that they could have been used as a mirror.

"Wonderful," Koenig said, his voice echoing through the cavernous chamber as he stood up. "I'm so glad you were able to accept my invitation."

Colt was struck by his confidence. The man was being held in a secret underground facility with no way of escape, and yet somehow he was still acting like he owned the place.

"Go on," Grandpa said, pointing for Colt to cross the bridge. "He can't get at you."

"Too true, I'm afraid," Koenig said.

"You've got exactly five minutes," the guard said.

"Thank you," Koenig said. "That should be more than enough time."

Colt felt a sensation like tiny fingers prodding at his thoughts, and he winced.

I can sense the monster raging inside of you, and yet you resist. Why? The voice belonged to Koenig, even though his lips hadn't moved.

"I don't know what you're talking about," Colt said, trying not to show that he was shaken.

"Let's not play games," Koenig said, this time aloud. "Thule blood courses through your veins, offering you unheard-of strength. Why not embrace it?"

Without realizing what he was doing, Colt reached for the medallion that hung around his neck. It was the same medallion Grandpa had worn during the Second World War, and it was inscribed with Psalm 46:1. *God is our refuge and strength, a very present help in trouble.*

Koenig laughed. "Yes, cry out to your God. But I wonder, where was he when the skies opened up and my brothers spilled the blood of thousands?"

"Let's go," Grandpa said, placing a strong but tender hand on Colt's shoulder.

"You won't win," Colt said, trying to sound confident. "By the time you figure out how to keep a gateway open long enough to let your armies through, we'll be ready."

"Pitiable," Koenig said. "Particularly since we both know that isn't true."

"Yes, it is," Colt said. "We found the schematics for the weapons you were developing at Trident Defense—including the particle destabilizer."

Koenig shook his head. "Those are merely experiments. Besides, even if by some miracle you were able to perfect them, you don't have time to put them into mass production—particularly since your mission launches on January 15."

Colt frowned.

"Why so surprised?" Koenig said. "Haven't you discovered

by now that you can read the thoughts of others? All Thule can. It's one of the many reasons we're superior to humans."

"Says the alien stuck in a cage."

"I didn't ask you here to match wits," Koenig said. "I simply want to make you an offer." He paused, his eyes locked on Colt's. "Join us and live."

"That's not much of an offer," Colt said. "Besides, Togarr— that's his name, right? You know, the warlord of the Black Sun Militia. He's making a play for supreme commander, which means your little treaty was broken."

"Togarr will be dealt with," Koenig said. "And our people will be united."

"If you say so."

"I've offered you an opportunity to live, and instead you mock me," Koenig said. "Know that it won't be long before this world will burn, and so will everyone in it."

"I won't let it happen."

Why? Because you're the Betrayer? Koenig said, his voice penetrating Colt's mind. *I can sense the change inside of you. Soon your body will be covered in scales. You'll be a hideous monster like the rest of us, and when that happens, humanity will turn on you. You'll be an outcast. A villain.*

Suddenly Colt felt a sharp pain in his temples, and before he realized what was happening, everything went black. The last thing he remembered was falling . . . and then he succumbed to the darkness.

CHAPTER 20

C olt opened his eyes to get his bearings, but whatever wasn't blurry was unbearably bright, so he closed them again. He had a splitting headache, and the constant tapping of someone pounding on a keyboard wasn't helping.

From what he could tell he was in a bed, but he was fairly certain that it wasn't his bunk back at the dorm. His nostrils burned with the smell of lemon, pine, and ammonia instead of the musty stench from the sheets that his roommates refused to wash.

"Is somebody going to tell me where I am?" he said through cracked lips, his voice weak.

"Good morning, sunshine."

"Oz?"

"Who did you expect, your fairy godmother?"

Colt opened his eyelids a slit and saw Oz standing at the

foot of his bed and Danielle sitting next to a window. "You didn't answer my question."

"You're in the campus infirmary, third floor," Danielle said. "And you're welcome. I mean, it's not like we've been cooped up in this place for the last thirty-six hours watching to make sure you didn't have a seizure or anything."

"A seizure? What happened?"

"Koenig pulled some kind of Jedi mind trick on you," Oz said. "One minute you were standing there, and the next minute you were out cold."

"Wait, were you there?" Colt asked, trying to reach back into his memory.

"Nah, but they showed us the video footage," Oz said. "At one point you were answering questions that Koenig never even asked. It was kind of crazy."

All Colt could remember was that Grandpa had taken him to an underground prison facility to meet Aldrich Koenig, but after that things got fuzzy.

"I don't get it," Colt said. "I mean, I thought you weren't allowed back on campus."

"Your grandpa pulled some strings," Oz said. "Apparently he doesn't think the campus security is good enough around here, so he wants me to watch your back."

"What strings did he pull?"

"The president was a big Phantom Flyer fan growing up," Danielle said. "So your grandpa promised him a signed picture in exchange for Oz's full reinstatement."

"He bribed him with an autograph?" Colt smiled as he shook his head.

"There were some stipulations," Oz said. "I had to agree to a full memory extraction to prove that I wasn't part of all that stuff my dad did. Plus I have to see a counselor once a week—you know, to talk about my feelings or whatever."

Colt had to stifle his laugh. "Seriously?"

"It isn't funny," Oz said. "I hate that stuff, but I did it for you. Figured you'd get yourself killed if I wasn't around."

"Does that mean you're back on Project Betrayal?"

"That's what they tell me," Oz said.

Colt felt relief wash over him. Knowing that his best friend was going to be there with him suddenly made success seem almost possible.

"So what happened in there?" Danielle said as she walked over and stood next to Oz. For a split second Colt could swear they were holding hands. "You know, with Koenig. Was he using telepathy or something?"

"To tell you the truth, I'm not sure," Colt said. "I could hear him—well, *feel* him inside my head. I tried to push him away, but I couldn't."

"I didn't know the Thule used telepathy," Danielle said.

"Then you need to read more," Oz said.

"I've read just about everything there is about them in the digital library."

"Try *The Phantom Flyer and the Agents of CHAOS* #87."

"That's right," Colt said as he sat up a little too quickly. He felt light-headed, and for a moment he thought that he was going to faint, but the sensation passed. "They had a spy network that infiltrated General MacArthur's staff, and they were leaking information telepathically to Thule scouts who were hiding nearby."

"Comic books aren't exactly the most reliable source when it comes to history," Danielle said.

"Says you," Oz said. "But it's true."

"Did you tell Dr. Roth?" Danielle asked.

Colt shook his head.

"Why not?"

"Probably because I've been unconscious," Colt said. "But I'm not sure if I want to tell him anyway."

"You can't keep secrets like that."

"Why, so they can dissect my brain to see if they can replicate whatever is happening to me? Because that's where this is heading."

"That's ridiculous."

"I don't know," Oz said. "He may be on to something."

Danielle shook her head. "You two are the biggest conspiracy theorists I've ever met."

"Takes one to know one," Oz said.

"How old are you?" Danielle asked.

"Look, as much as I love listening to the two of you bicker like an old married couple, I have a splitting headache. Think you can find me some aspirin?"

"I might have something even better," Danielle said. "That is, if you're up to it."

iiiiiiiiiiiiiiiiiiiiiiiiiiiiiii

Colt couldn't believe it. Somehow Danielle had managed to get Lily Westcott in front of a hologram camera. Her image was standing in front of him looking as real as if she were right there in the room.

He reached out and touched the empty air that was her hand, and she leaned forward and kissed him on the cheek. Even though it was only a hologram, it felt so real.

"What happened to your hair?" she said, her perfect lips parted in a smile.

Colt rubbed his hand over the stubble. "Do you like it?"

"I'm not going to lie," she said as the smile disappeared. "I liked it long. But you still look handsome."

The smile returned, and Colt felt actual warmth erupt inside his chest.

"Mostly I'm just glad you're still alive."

"Look, I want to apologize for the way things ended back home," he said, bowing his head to look at the ground. "I shouldn't have left you alone, and then they arrested you and—"

Colt still felt guilty for abandoning Lily at the rodeo the night before he left for the CHAOS Academy. He had wanted to tell her how he felt—that he really cared about her, maybe even loved her—but then he got into a fight with a shape-shifting alien, and before he knew what was happening, he was detained by agents from the Department of Alien Affairs. Since Lily was there with him, she got detained as well.

"It's okay," she said. "I mean . . . maybe at first I was a little upset."

"A little?"

"A lot," she said, but she was smiling. "Your grandpa came over and explained what happened, though."

"He did?"

She smiled, and Colt longed to take her in his arms. "He told us everything."

"I should have called you. I wanted to apologize, but . . ." His voice trailed off as she stepped close enough that Colt imagined he could feel her breath on his cheek.

"All I wanted was to hear that you were all right. That *we* were all right."

He touched his fingers to her holographic cheek, remembering how soft her skin was. "I didn't want to make it harder than it already was."

"I pray for you every night." Her voice was barely a whisper.

"Me too." He stopped to consider what he had just said. "I mean, I pray for you. Not me."

They both laughed.

"I know this might sound strange," she said. "But let's not talk. Let's just be here together for a little while. Okay?"

Colt nodded, savoring each moment.

:: CHAPTER 21 ::

olt stood in one of the tunnels beneath Tesla Stadium waiting for his cue to take the field with the rest of the flight team. He could see members of the Virginia Tech marching band as they performed a medley of songs from the original *Star Wars* soundtrack in front of a capacity crowd that had grown well beyond standing room only.

Three thousand more had gathered outside the gates of the academy, all hoping to catch even a glimpse of the historic moment when the Phantom Flyer and his Agents of CHAOS would take to the skies for the first time in over fifty years.

Becoming the official symbol of hope in the fight against the Thule should have made Colt nervous. The president of the United States was going to be in attendance, along with a laundry list of politicians, corporate leaders, musicians, and actors, and all of them wanted to meet him after the show. And everything was going to be broadcast in more than two hundred countries and thirty languages, to a viewership that was supposed to eclipse one hundred million. But all he could think about was Lily Westcott. Her eyes. Her smile. Even the scent of her shampoo.

He wanted to slip away and head back to Arizona right then and there, but the campus was swarming with agents from the CIA, FBI, DAA, and Secret Service, not to mention the heavily armed members of Delta Force. They were all there to make sure nothing happened to Colt, which meant that all eyes were on him.

"Looks like the president's motorcade has arrived," Colt heard Captain Starling announce through the speakers inside his helmet.

"You mean his body double?" Oz said.

There were rumors that the president had employed a team of shape-shifting Thule to stand in for him during any public appearances, while he and his family hid in an underground bunker—which seemed odd, considering that all of humanity was at war with the Thule.

"I can pretty much guarantee you that the Secret Service is monitoring this frequency, genius," Danielle said.

Oz shrugged. "What are they going to do, arrest me for telling the truth? Besides, if they haven't locked me away by now, I doubt it's ever going to happen."

The sound of footsteps echoed through the tunnel, and when Colt turned around he saw three men in black suits and mirrored sunglasses, each with a white earpiece and a stoic expression.

"Told you they were listening," Danielle said, but the Secret Service agents walked past Oz.

"Cadet McAlister?" the lead agent asked as he approached Colt. He was older than the other two, with cropped gray hair and skin so pale that Colt wondered if he was a vampire.

Oz, who had never been much for diplomacy, stood in front of Colt with his arms folded across his massive chest. "Who wants to know?"

"My name is Agent Marz, and this is Agent Denton. The gentleman with the briefcase is Agent Galloway." He paused a moment, as though waiting for Oz to introduce himself, but he didn't. "We're going to need Cadet McAlister to remove his helmet and one of his gloves."

"I don't think so," Oz said.

Agent Marz was at least six inches shorter and thirty pounds lighter than Oz, but if he was intimidated, he didn't show it. "Please step aside, son."

"Uh-oh," Danielle said, her voice barely a whisper as it carried over the comlink. "This is about to get ugly."

Oz narrowed his eyes and flared his nostrils. "I'm not your son," he said, the words spilling from his lips like a growl.

"What's going on down there?" Captain Starling said through his comlink.

"We have a bit of an issue," Glyph said, the pitch of his voice betraying his nerves. "Members of the Secret Service have arrived, and they are asking—"

"Yes, I heard what they asked," Captain Starling said. "What I want to know is why."

"Excuse me," Glyph said, raising his unusually long index

finger as he shuffled toward the agents. "I hate to be a bother, but Captain Starling—he's the . . . I'm sorry, I've forgotten the title that he asked us to use."

"Executive producer," Danielle said, rolling her eyes.

"Ah, yes," Glyph said with a nod. "The executive producer of the show would like to inquire as to the nature of your business with Cadet McAlister."

"According to our records, we've tested the entire campus, with one exception."

Colt's eyes went wide, and his heart started to thrum behind his rib cage. The Secret Service had arrived early that morning to run everyone from cadets and instructors to dishwashers and maintenance workers through a series of tests to determine if any shapeshifters had infiltrated the campus prior to the president's arrival.

Colt's status as the next Phantom Flyer was public knowledge, but the fact that Thule DNA flowed through his bloodstream was not. The last thing the government wanted was for the American people to find out that their savior was anything but human, and Superintendent Thorne had assured Colt that he wouldn't be tested. Apparently Agent Marz didn't get the memo.

"Where's Superintendent Thorne?" Captain Starling asked, his voice borderline shrill.

Colt could picture his face turning red and the veins in his neck starting to pop out.

"What about Giru Ba or Lohr? Please tell me there's a faculty member down there with you."

"Not at the moment," Glyph said, his head swiveling on his long neck as he searched the room.

"This is a disaster," Captain Starling said. "Whatever you do, don't let them run that test, and that's an order. Do you hear me?"

"Um . . . sir, does that mean you're asking us to engage in conflict?" Glyph asked.

"That's exactly what he's asking," Oz said, dropping his arms as his hands formed into fists. "So listen, Agent Marz, is it?" He took a step toward the agent. "I'm afraid you and your clones are going to have to leave. We're about to put on a show for the entire world, and you're kind of breaking our concentration."

"That won't be possible," Agent Marz said. "Please step aside."

"That's not going to happen."

"I won't tell you again."

"Is that supposed to be a threat?" Oz said as the flight team surrounded the Secret Service agents, each of them in full fight gear.

"All we need is a blood sample," Agent Marz said as he opened the left side of his jacket, revealing a handgun in a chest holster.

"Fine," Colt said, removing his glove as he pushed past Oz. He'd already lost his parents, and he was about to watch his friends get shot because they were trying to make sure his secret didn't get out.

"What are you doing?" Oz reached out and grabbed Colt by the shoulder, but Colt pulled away. "It's not going to happen."

"That's enough."

Everyone turned to see Murdoch McAlister walk through the door, followed by Superintendent Thorne and Giru Ba.

"Finally," Oz said. "Will you tell these jerks that—"

"I said that's enough, and I meant it," Grandpa said, cutting him off.

"Agent Marz, I'm afraid you won't be able to test Cadet McAlister today for reasons that I'm unable to discuss," Superintendent Thorne said.

"With all due respect—"

"I understand that you have a job to do," she said, raising her hand to cut him off. "But if you check with your supervisor, you'll see that the order comes from an authority greater than all of us."

"God told you not to test his blood?" Glyph said, the awe in his voice unmistakable.

The usually unflappable director started to smile. "No, Cadet Glyph. The directive came from the Office of the President."

"It checks out," Agent Denton said, and Colt felt all of the tension leave his body.

:: CHAPTER 22 ::

"Tell me why we're doing this again," Colt said, feeling nervous for the first time as he listened to the crowd chant, "Phan-tom Fly-er! Phan-tom Fly-er!" over and over.

"Because people need a symbol of hope," Danielle said. "And like it or not, that's you."

Colt was uncomfortable with all the adulation, but at least they weren't chanting, "Betrayer! Betrayer!" He looked over at his grandfather, who was standing with his arms folded across his chest as he listened to a conversation between Superintendent Thorne and Giru Ba. Grandpa was everything that the Phantom Flyer was supposed to be. Tall with broad shoulders and a wide jaw. Confident. Unflappable. *He* was what the world needed, not a sixteen-year-old kid who had no idea what he was doing.

"Can you see the president?" Grey asked, peeking over Colt's shoulder.

"Not from here," Oz said when Colt didn't answer. "But I'm pretty sure he's up in the press box behind that wall of bullet-proof glass. And it looks like Pierce's dad is right up there with him. Making sure he's getting in all the photos."

A single snare drum rattled, and a hush went over the crowd as Colt watched four marines in dress uniform escort a girl to the middle of the field. She wore a formfitting dress covered in gold sequins that shimmered beneath the lights. Spiraling blond hair bounced with each step, and there was something about the way she walked . . . It was familiar, but it was also impossible.

"Lily?"

Colt's heart raced as he watched her follow the marines up onto a dais, and as she stepped up to the microphone and sang the first five words, he knew that it was Lily singing "The Star-Spangled Banner."

"Why didn't you tell me?" Colt said to no one in particular.

"I didn't know," Danielle said.

"Me either," Oz said. "Just make sure you keep your head in the game. I don't care what they say about these flight suits, if you crash at a hundred feet, you're not walking away."

"She's amazing," Stacy said.

"Yeah, she is," Colt said, savoring every note.

Cameras flashed in an erratic sequence like fireflies lighting up a summer night as the song hit the crescendo, but when it ended there was an odd silence. Then someone whistled and a few people started to clap. Before long everyone in the stadium was standing and cheering.

"Okay, everyone, it's showtime!" Captain Starling said.

Fireworks exploded, showering the night sky in a burst of

color as smoke machines at the mouth of the tunnel whirred to life. Smoke issued from the tubes, rising like fog over a swamp as the crowd continued to cheer.

"Ten seconds," Captain Starling said.

"Do you think she's transferring?" Colt said as he watched her stand there smiling at the cheering crowd.

"Here? Yeah, right," Oz said. "What's she going to do, sing for the Thule?"

"I know it's hard, but don't be a jerk," Danielle said.

Captain Starling started his countdown. "Five . . . four . . ."

The snare drum started to beat again, and Lily followed the marines back down the steps. She hesitated when she got to the bottom, and for a moment it appeared like she was looking at Colt. A gust of wind buffeted her hair, and she reached up to pull back a strand that had fallen across her forehead.

"Three . . . two . . ."

She walked away, across the field and back into the shadows of a tunnel. Colt felt empty and alone, and when he looked down at his uniform, he suddenly felt like a fraud. There was no way people were going to believe that he was the reincarnation of the Phantom Flyer. He was too short. Too young. Too scared.

"One!"

Oz was the first one out of the tunnel, hefting an enormous American flag in his hands as he sprinted to the center of the field. The rest of the flight team followed, and as the smoke swirled around them, Colt imagined that they were the original Agents of CHAOS running out to meet the Nazis somewhere in the Ardennes.

"Where's the star of our show?" Captain Starling asked as the public address announcer introduced the Agents of CHAOS.

Colt took a last look at Grandpa, who nodded. "This is your time," Grandpa said, as though he could hear the doubts swirling in Colt's mind. "Go out there and make us proud."

A litany of excuses rushed through Colt like raging water. They formed on his tongue and pressed to escape through his lips, but instead he took a deep breath and exhaled slowly. "Thanks." A simple word, but it was all he had to offer.

Bright lights flashed through the stands as Oz slammed the flagpole into the ground. The crowd was raucous as he stood there with his hands on his hips and his feet set wide, striking a classic superhero pose as the Stars and Stripes snapped in the wind behind him. "Let's go, McAlister," he said through his comlink.

"It looks like you have things under control," Colt said, smiling as he shook his head. Oz was improvising, and Colt was fairly certain that Captain Starling was about to have an aneurysm.

"That's off script," Starling said as though on cue. "Colt, can you hear me? Colt . . . Colt?"

"I can hear you, sir."

"Are you waiting for an invitation or something? Get out there!"

"Yes, sir." Colt ran down the tunnel and out onto the airfield. The sun was long gone, but the stadium lights flared bright enough that Colt had to shield his eyes, even with the tinted visor on his helmet.

"It's about time," Oz said as trumpets sounded and snare drums snapped.

The crowd grew frenzied, and Colt wondered if this was

what the quarterback of a Super Bowl team felt like when he ran onto the field before the game. The emotions were strange. Excitement. Embarrassment. Pride. Awe. And for a moment it was hard to breathe.

"Ladies and gentlemen . . . the Phantom Flyer!"

Colt raised his right hand and waved to the crowd. The stadium shook as the people stamped their feet and clapped their hands, and Colt knew that whatever was happening, it wasn't about him. They weren't looking for someone to save them; they wanted to be inspired, to believe that they could overcome. They wanted hope.

"Wait for it," Captain Starling said.

Rockets hissed as fireworks shot into the sky. Smoke trailed behind, and when the rockets reached three hundred feet they hung in the air, but only for a moment. The first rocket burst, sending streams of red light showering through the darkness. Another exploded, this one white. Then another. Blue. They continued to erupt, lighting the night in a brilliant display.

"And go!" Captain Starling said.

As one, the Phantom Flyer and his Agents of CHAOS ignited their jet packs. Colt hit the thrust, and fiery exhaust spit from his engines. Even through his armor he could feel the heat against his legs and lower back as his feet left the ground. Power surged and Colt rose, arms tight against his body and toes pointed as he looked up at the sliver of moon that hung in the sky.

The Agents of CHAOS formed a perfect circle around him, and as they climbed, the frenzied sounds of the crowd faded. Soon the stadium looked like nothing more than a toy that was small enough to fit in Colt's palm.

"Ladies and gentlemen, the starburst!"

As Colt rose, he slowly spun, and his exhaust trail formed a corkscrew. The other pilots veered away, their own exhaust bending as they cascaded back toward the stadium. Colt extended his arms and arched his back like he was diving backward into a swimming pool, and when the crown of his head was pointed at the ground, he pulled his arms to his body and increased throttle, heading back toward the stadium like a falling star.

The Agents of CHAOS flew maneuver after maneuver, cutting across the stadium in a diamond pattern and then a V. They shot straight up, weaving in and out until the tails from their exhausts twined to form what looked like a giant length of rope. They flew backward and upside down, did barrel rolls and arching loops, spins and dives.

Colt pulled away from one formation and took a pass over the crowd. They cheered, jumping up and down and waving, but none of that mattered. He was looking for one person. When he finally spotted Lily, she was seated next to Grandpa in the box seats next to the railing. She looked beautiful; her hair danced in the wind and her blue eyes sparkled as they reflected the stadium lights.

"I thought we talked about this," Captain Starling said as cameras flashed all around. "It's important that we stick to the script."

Colt ignored him as he raced toward Lily, every eye in the stadium following. He pulled up and hovered in place, wondering if any of this was real. There she was, not more than five feet away. Colt wanted to pick her up in his arms and fly away, but that would have to wait.

"Hi," he said, feeling both awkward and elated.

"Hi."

"I'm kind of in the middle of something, but I was wondering if you wanted to hang out after this. I mean, unless you're busy."

Her face flushed red as she smiled. "Like a date?"

"Yeah, like a date." Colt was thankful that she couldn't see his face, because now it was his turn to blush.

"Then I accept."

"Ahem." Captain Starling cleared his voice. "Cadet, if you're finished, we have a show to put on."

:: CHAPTER 23 ::

L adies and gentlemen," said the public address announcer, "please welcome Mother Russia's very own Crimson Bear!"

The crowd cheered as Pierce flew into the stadium and shot toward Colt, who barely managed to get out of the way.

"What are you doing?" Colt asked.

"What does it look like I'm doing, genius?" Pierce pulled in front of the grandstand and bowed in midair. He basked in the applause before turning back around and rumbling toward Colt, amber eyes blazing as the exhaust burst from the bottom of his boots.

Colt opened the throttle, and Pierce gave chase as the crowd cheered them on. Everything was a blur, but as Colt darted around the aerial field he thought he saw Robert Downey Jr. sitting next to Scarlett Johansson in the loge section, along with George Lucas, Harrison Ford, and all four judges from *The Voice*. "Wait, is that—"

"Yeah, it's Charlize Theron," Oz said, cutting him off. "But you might want to focus on Bowen."

Colt turned his head in time to see that he was about to fly into the press box where VIPs like Senator Bowen and the president of the United States were supposed to be watching them. He released the throttle and arched his head back, changing his trajectory so that he shot straight up, and that's when he saw the sky open up.

The Hydra looked like a flying aircraft carrier as it emerged from the portal, light dancing across the surface. It had a hangar, eight rotors that kept it aloft, and two long flight decks filled with dozens of Taipan fighters.

"What is that thing?" Pierce asked as he pulled up beside Colt, who was hovering near a green flag decorated with the familiar symbol of the Department of Alien Affairs: a white hand with three long fingers.

"A Delta Class Hydra, which means there could be a thousand Thule on board, not to mention twenty Taipan."

"What about those?"

Colt looked up to see three massive figures drop from the sky. They were little more than specks at first, but as they neared the ground, he could see that each one was at least thirty feet tall and wrapped in a thick iron hide.

"Trackers!" Oz shouted as the first landed, sending a tremor across the entire campus.

People rushed out of the stadium in a blind panic as the second Tracker landed near the first. The third Tracker landed outside the stadium, amber eyes glowing like spotlights as its head swiveled as though it was searching the campus grounds.

Colt hovered, watching the events unfold like a spectator in someone else's nightmare. A Thule transport landed nearby; the hatch opened, and at least twenty-six armed aliens poured out.

The crowd was screaming. Colt prayed that Grandpa McAlister had gotten Lily to safety as DAA agents opened fire on the Thule, who attacked in kind. One of the agents flew in on a jet pack and shot a rocket launcher that hit the Tracker in its knee, but it only left a burn mark.

Colt looked up again and saw three Apache helicopters release Hellfire missiles that pounded the Tracker. It staggered but somehow kept its feet and answered the attack with a hail of missiles that erupted from the launcher on its shoulder.

One hit an Apache, piercing the hull. Fire and smoke billowed as the helicopter fell, spinning slowly until it hit the ground.

"I saw Lily," Oz said. "She followed a bunch of people into the admin building."

"On it," Colt said as he flew over the top of the stadium and out toward the campus grounds. Thanks to the jet pack, it didn't take long to reach the front steps of the administration building. He looked around for anything he could use as a weapon and saw a DAA agent facedown, his hand still wrapped around the barrel of an assault rifle.

Colt approached cautiously, knowing it could be a trap. He tapped the agent with the tip of his boot; the man didn't budge, so he tried again. Nothing. Heart pounding, he picked up the assault rifle, but the magazine was empty.

The hair on the back of his neck stood on end as he listened to the faint echoes of someone screaming. He tossed the assault rifle on the steps, knelt beside the fallen agent, and unlatched the holster that held the man's handgun. Colt half expected him to stand up, or at least to reach out and grab his wrist, but he didn't budge.

"Thank you." Colt wanted to say more, to thank him for sacrificing his life. He wondered if the man had children, and how they would react once they learned that their father was dead.

Another scream. The sound of something heavy crashing against the floor. Colt felt the weight of the gun in his hand and remembered what Grandpa had said, that there was no glory in killing. Did that go for the Thule as well? Did they have hopes and dreams, or were they soulless killing machines?

He slipped inside the building, the gun held to his chest as his eyes searched the reception area. There were splatters of green liquid on the ground, which he assumed was blood from the Thule. A trail of drops led toward Director Thorne's office. Colt removed the magazine from the handgun to make sure it was full; then he checked the chamber and found an extra round, which meant that he had thirteen shots. It wasn't enough to take down one of the Thule unless he got lucky and hit it in the eye, but it was better than nothing.

Two more DAA agents were lying on the floor in the hallway. "God is our refuge and strength, a very present help in trouble," Colt whispered, reciting the verse from Grandpa's medallion as he hurried past an empty office.

"McAlister!"

Colt spun, his heart pounding in his chest. He found Pierce crouched beneath two bookshelves that had fallen at odd angles. "What are you doing?" Colt asked.

"Looking for my dad, so shut up and get in here before one of those things hears you."

There was a sound like shuffling feet, and Colt turned to see something heavy moving slowly toward them from the other end of the hallway. He could only make out its silhouette, but it was well over seven feet tall with six muscular arms and a long tail that swished back and forth. It stopped to sniff the air.

"You see one, don't you?" Pierce said.

Colt nodded.

"Anybody else with you?"

"It's just me," Colt said.

"We need to go find backup."

"Not without Lily."

"The girl you were flirting with back at the stadium? She was hot."

Colt fought the urge to break Pierce's jaw.

"Relax," Pierce said. "I'm not going to hit on her or anything."

"Lucky me."

A Thule bellowed, and the hideous sound reverberated through the hallway.

"We can't stay here," Colt said.

"I can't just let them take my dad."

"Then let's go find him."

Pierce narrowed his eyes. "Seriously? You'd help me?"

"We can help each other. Let's go."

Colt and Pierce followed the trail of blood to Director Thorne's office, where a fake bookshelf had been ripped away from the wall, revealing what looked like elevator doors.

"I don't get it," Pierce said. "This is a one-story building."

Colt had a terrible thought. "Koenig."

||||||||||||||||||||||||||||||||

Pierce had a hard time believing that the United States government was housing the leader of the Thule under the academy grounds, but he followed Colt into the elevator and down to the same floor where Grandpa had taken Colt.

"Hold on." Colt heard a faint whisper.

Closer, closer, the voice said. *Show no mercy. Kill them. Free me.*

"What's wrong?" Pierce asked.

"We're getting close," Colt said.

"What, you have some kind of super-powered hearing now?"

"Something like that." He wasn't about to tell Pierce that he could hear Koenig speaking in his head.

When the elevator stopped and the door opened, they found a man in a dark suit lying on the ground moaning, a ring of blood staining the tile around his head. "Who . . . who's there?" he asked, his voice faint as he struggled to lift his head.

"Captain Starling?" Colt ran toward the instructor.

Starling looked up at him, eyes filled with terror even as he forced a smile. His skin was pale, his hair wild, and his right arm had been severed at the elbow. "Trust me, it hurts worse than it looks," he said through a coughing fit.

"It's not that bad," Colt said.

Starling looked down at the bloody stump, and for a moment it looked like he was going to cry. "I tried to stop them," he said, closing his eyes. "But they were . . ." His voice broke off into sobs.

"It's okay," Colt said, kneeling beside him.

"He's lost a lot of blood," Pierce said.

"I know." He looked around, trying to find something that he could use as a tourniquet, but there weren't many options. "We're going to get you out of here, but first we need to stop the bleeding. Okay?"

Starling nodded.

"This might hurt." Colt reached up and ripped the sleeve from Starling's flight suit, trying not to gag as the stench of blood filled his nostrils. Starling groaned as Colt cinched the sleeve around the injured arm.

"Thank you," he said, and then his body went limp.

Colt pressed his fingers just below Starling's jaw, but he couldn't feel a pulse.

"Is he dead?" Piercc asked.

"Yeah," Colt said, reaching to close Starling's eyelids. He shook his head, wondering if any of this was real. Starling was an annoying blowhard who drove everyone crazy, but Colt wouldn't have wished this in a million years.

"Now what?" Pierce said.

Colt stood up and wiped his hands on his armor, leaving streaks of blood that matched the streaks on the biometric scanner. He led Pierce to Koenig's detention cell and stopped short. The cell was open, and two DAA agents were lying still on the ground.

"Looks like they already—"

Before Colt could finish his sentence, a massive Thule rushed out of the room and grabbed him by the throat. It hefted him off the ground.

I like to watch the life pour out of the eyes when people die, don't you?

A cold hand caressed Colt's mind. Koenig.

"Let him go!" Pierce raised his M14, but Koenig only laughed.

Or what?

A feral sound escaped from between Colt's lips as he lashed out, catching the Thule in the throat. It bellowed, releasing him as Pierce opened fire. Bullets sprayed, covering Koenig. He stepped back and Colt lunged, trying to take its legs out.

Ah, sweet rage. Do you not see how it empowers us? It makes us stronger, so nothing can stand against us!

"I'm nothing like you!" Colt screamed as he pounded Koenig's jaw with his fists.

That's it. Let it flow. Embrace what you've become.

As the beast within threatened to take over, Colt fought to hold on to his humanity. *My name is Colt McAlister. My parents were Mary and Roger McAlister. My grandpa's name is Murdoch McAlister, and my best friends are Oz Romero and Danielle Salazar.*

Surrender and live.

"Never."

Then behold your destiny.

Before Koenig could move, Colt grabbed his jaw. Koenig shook his head and flung Colt against the wall. Pain shot down Colt's spine as Koenig sprang and, in one quick motion, ripped Colt's helmet from his head.

Look for the soft spot, Colt thought.

Koenig bit down on Colt's shoulder, and his teeth cut through the skin of Colt's neck. Searing pain was followed by nausea, and for a moment Colt thought he was going to pass out.

Gunfire. A flash of light, and the Thule cried out. He burst past them and ran down the hall toward the elevator.

:: CHAPTER 24 ::

The Trackers had destroyed half of the academy's campus before air strikes took them out. By last count five Secret Service agents, twelve agents from the DAA, and thirty-four spectators were dead. The injured were too numerous to count.

The commissary had become a makeshift triage where Dr. Roth and his medibots, along with a handful of medical volunteers who had been sitting in the stands, applied bandages, set broken bones, and attempted surgical procedures without the necessary tools—including anesthesia.

Colt lay on a table looking up at Dr. Roth, but he could see Grandpa leaning against a pillar out of the corner of his eye. "Did they find Koenig?" he asked, nausea churning in his stomach.

"Not yet," Grandpa said.

"What about Lily?"

"She's a bit scared, but she'll be fine."

"I need you to stop talking," Dr. Roth said through his surgical mask as he poked at the bite marks on Colt's neck. "Does that hurt?"

"I thought I wasn't supposed to talk," Colt said through the pain.

"Answer the man," Grandpa said.

"Yeah, it hurts. Is it infected or something?"

"The scans show increased activity in the part of your brain that controls aggression, and we think it's due to a virus that was passed into your system when Koenig bit you."

"What does that mean?" Colt said.

Dr. Roth looked over at Grandpa, who nodded. "I'm afraid the change is accelerating," he said.

Colt felt the panic rise as he pictured four extra arms growing out of his back, not to mention a tail. He ran his tongue across his teeth to see if they were sharp, and he looked down at his hands and feet, wondering if his body was covered in scales.

"Relax," Dr. Roth said.

"Relax? You're not the one who's turning into a monster."

"I think I can help. That is, if you'll let me."

"How?"

"I'd like to introduce a mixture of interferon and some other viral agents that I believe will slow it down."

Colt took a series of shallow breaths. His mouth was dry. "Fine," he said. He didn't want to play the part of the guinea pig, but he was even more scared of becoming a monster. Panic welled inside of him, threatening to burst like an overripe thundercloud. His jaw clenched so tight that it started to spasm, and he didn't even realize that he had bit his own tongue. His mouth filled with the iron taste of blood. Distant thoughts, familiar yet strange, flooded his memory.

He was five years old, and he was in an examination room strapped to a table. Terror made his heart flutter like a hummingbird that had overdosed on sugar. He fought to break free, but the straps were too strong.

"It's okay . . . we're right here." It was his mother, and though her words had been meant to reassure him, the fear in her voice had the opposite effect. He fought even harder, desperate to break free, and he was certain that his mother was crying, though she was trying to hide it.

"He'll be fine," Colt's father said, trying to offer strength. Even his voice was laced with an uncertainty that Colt had never heard before.

Someone—a doctor, or maybe another lab technician—walked into view. The details of his face were obscured, but Colt would never forget that smile. It wasn't kind, or genuine, for that matter. It was the kind of smile that a salesman offers when he knows he has tricked you into buying something you don't need or want.

"Just relax," the man had said. "It'll be over before you know it."

God is our refuge and strength, a very present help in trouble.

The cry of the wounded broke into his memories. Deep in his blood, the alien DNA had hold of him. The temptation to enjoy the sound of suffering was immense and sickening. The bile in his stomach threatened to crawl up his throat and out his mouth.

God is our refuge and strength, a very present help in trouble.

Was Colt meant to be the strength of his people, and of all the good and peaceful aliens who wanted to resist the Thule? What if all the hope the military had placed in him was for nothing? What if he failed, and all the people he cared about were lost?

What if he lost his soul in the stew of fury and rage that marked the Thule?

God is our refuge and strength, a very present help in trouble.

A sensation like fire burned through his veins, starting in his shoulder and traveling across his body. His fingers and toes went numb and his tongue started to swell, filling his mouth and making it impossible to swallow, much less breathe.

God is our refuge and strength, a very present help in trouble.

Images flashed in Colt's head. His mom kissing him good night. The first time his dad took him surfing. Sitting in his grandfather's lap as he read stories from the Bible. Fishing with Danielle when they were eleven. Playing *Zombie Exterminator* with Oz. Listening to Lily sing and play the guitar. Walking Stacy home the other night.

A feral scream exploded from Colt's lips. He sat up, arms flexed and head thrown back as he suffered pain unlike anything he had experienced in his life. Fire blazed through his body and heat radiated through his skin. All he could do was cry out, though the bellow sounded foreign to his ears. It was like a wild beast gone mad. His muscles shrieked and flesh burned as shadowy figures rushed toward him.

Chaos. Pain. Hopelessness. Death had to be near. Humans weren't made to suffer like this.

Colt wanted to apologize for failing them—for failing

mankind. He was a fraud, not some savior. He'd known that all along. Why would God have chosen someone like him—someone so frail? Oz. He was the right choice. Or Grey or Stacy.

Colt felt his body go stiff and he fell back, struggling—gasping for each breath. He clutched the fabric of the thin sheet atop the table in his balled fists.

"What's going on?" Was that his father? No, his father was dead. His grandfather was saying, "Get that medication into him before we lose him."

Paddles were slammed against his chest. The steel felt cold against his burning skin as muddled thoughts gave way to clarity. Colt knew that he was going to die, and strange as it seemed, that was fine. No, it was wonderful. He knew that he had never belonged—that his time on earth was nothing more than a layover—a precursor to an eternity that promised a peace that this world could never know. There were no regrets. No longings. Only quiet contentment.

Electricity burst across the paddles and into his chest. His back arched and his body shook.

"Again! Get the antiviral ready."

Another burst of pain. Colt's eyes shot open and he gasped for breath.

"See there," Dr. Roth said. "I knew the good Lord wasn't ready to take you—not yet anyway. This war isn't over."

:: CHAPTER 25 ::

Senator Bowen lay on a table, unconscious. The stump of his left leg was wrapped in bloody bandages where it was missing from the knee down.

"He's going to make it," Stacy said. She was sitting across the room, plastic tubing running from the crook of her elbow into a plastic bag that was rapidly filling with blood. "He just needs some blood before they can transport him out of here."

"What kind?" Colt asked.

"Not yours."

He frowned.

"Look, even if the needles could puncture your skin—which they can't—your blood is . . . well, you know."

"Contaminated?"

"Different."

In other words, I'm a freak, Colt thought to himself. "Have you seen Pierce?"

Stacy frowned and looked away, her eyes focused squarely on the linoleum floor.

"What's wrong?"

"Nothing. It's just that . . . well, he's out looking for the rest of his dad's leg."

"Where?"

"The stadium."

Colt started to walk out the door, but Stacy grabbed his hand.

"Wait," she said. "I need to tell you something."

His heart started to pound.

She took a deep breath. "This is totally embarrassing, so I'm just going to come out and say it," she said. "I need to apologize."

"For what?"

"I know you still have feelings for Lily and . . . well, I need to respect that," she said. "Danielle told me that you two are perfect for each other, and I don't want to get caught in the middle of it. It's not fair to either one of you." She pulled him toward her and kissed him on his forehead. "Good night."

||||||||||||||||||||||||||||||||

Numb, Colt thought as he walked down the path back toward his dorm. Numb to the touch of Stacy's lips. Numb to the devastation on the campus. Numb to the storm of sirens and flashing lights. Numb to the body bags.

The skin of his soul thickened with the skin of his body. *And this,* he thought, *this is how the Thule did it*—a singular focus on the mission set before them and no extra thought or feeling or pain given to anything except that mission. He knew what their fury tasted like. It sat in the back of his throat now, metallic and strangely sweet. Pain was only spice to this sugar, devastation like yeast.

"No! Please, no!"

Colt stopped when he heard Glyph's voice cut through the cool mist.

"I'm not one of them," Glyph said. "I'm . . . please. You can't."

Colt ran off the path and into a grove, where he saw Glyph backed against a tree. Pierce was holding a gun to the alien's midsection, which according to their xenology textbook was where the Fimorian brain was located.

"What are you doing, Bowen?"

"Back off, McAlister!" Pierce said without so much as looking at him.

"Please . . . ," Glyph said, his voice weak.

"He's on our side."

"No, he's not. He's one of them!"

"I'm more Thule than he is, so if you want to shoot someone, why don't you shoot me?" Colt walked toward Pierce with his arms held wide to show that he wasn't armed.

"Don't tempt me," Pierce said.

"Your dad is going to make it," Colt said, each step slow and methodical. "They're moving him to Fort Meade. Doc Roth even said they could get him a prosthetic that will look and act like the real thing. It even has nerve endings."

"I know what you're trying to do, and it won't work."

"Listen, just give me the—"

"Shut up, okay? Just shut up!"

Glyph winced as he closed his eyes.

"The universe is bigger than we thought," Colt said, trying to keep a steady voice. "But that doesn't mean everyone and everything out there is our enemy."

"Think, McAlister. Sooner or later they're all going to turn on us."

"No, we won't," Glyph said, his voice feeble as a tear ran down his cheek. "Please, we came to help you in your fight. You . . . you must believe me."

"Liar." Pierce curled his lip into a snarl.

Colt leapt. He snatched the weapon away, tossed it, and had his fist cocked to flatten Pierce when Glyph called out, "No. Don't. He's scared, that's all."

Pierce exploded, but not in anger. Sobs, so consuming Colt thought the cadet would rip his lungs out. Glyph's long arm snaked around Pierce's ribs and he pulled him tight. "Come," he said. "Let's go find your father."

Pierce nodded and let Glyph lead them in the direction of the commissary.

:: **CHAPTER 26** ::

A s news of the attack spread, people around the world
fled dense population centers in search of somewhere to
hide. The Black Hills. The Gobi Desert. Pitcairn Island.
Even the boreal forest of Canada, which was supposed to be
uninhabitable in the winter.

Some tried to pack things like precious jewels and fur
coats, afraid that looters would break into their homes, but
most stuck to canned goods, water bottles, and weapons that
ranged from baseball bats and butcher knives to hunting rifles
and handguns.

Colt and Oz sat in Grandpa's apartment, watching a reporter
from one of the twenty-four-hour news networks interview
Senator Bowen in his hospital bed. His hair was perfect, his
teeth almost too white, and his skin looked orange from all the
makeup. But his eyes were heavy and his voice was weak.

"Check it out," Oz said. "Pierce is in the background. See him?"

"Yeah, I see him," Colt said.

The reporter asked the senator about the attack and what his first thought was when he saw the Tracker, but when she asked him about the rumors of his affair with the Secretary of State, Pierce cut it short.

"No way!" Oz shouted as he watched Pierce knock the camera out of the cameraman's hands. It fell to the floor, bouncing as it continued to record Pierce's boots and a litany of colorful language as he threatened to drop the reporter through a portal if she didn't leave.

"That was classic," Oz said as the broadcast went to commercial. "I mean, not that I blame him. But can you believe that?"

"It was stupid," Colt said as he flipped through the channels. "People are going to see his uniform and think we're all like that."

"People are going to see a son standing up for his dad," Oz said.

"Whatever." Colt stopped when he saw aerial footage of the Manhattan Bridge. The lanes that led into Manhattan were empty, but cars were stacked across the lanes leading out, and none of them was moving. People were getting out of their cars and running. Most didn't bother shutting their doors. "We should be there helping them."

"The National Guard is already there," Oz said. "Besides, the Army Corps of Engineers couldn't build a bridge fast enough to help them. What would we do?"

"Anything is better than sitting around here waiting for orders."

"You won't have to worry about that much longer." Grandpa walked into the room holding two plates stacked high with roast beef sandwiches on rye, pickle spears, and Ruffles potato chips. "We're packing up and heading west."

"Back to Arizona?"

Grandpa shook his head. "The federal government is moving to what the Joint Chiefs of Staff believe is a more defensible position, west of the Rockies. The cadets of CHAOS Academy are part of the security staff that's going to protect the caravan—only you aren't cadets any longer. You've all been given field promotions."

"What, so we're generals now?" Oz said.

"Not quite," Grandpa said. "They've come up with a new title. Junior Agent."

By the look on his face, it appeared as though Oz just finished smelling a bag of week-old gym socks. "Junior Agents? That's lame."

"You also get live ammunition," Grandpa said. "And you get paid."

"How much?"

"It won't really matter if we don't find a way to stop the lizard men," Grandpa said as he set the plates on the coffee table in front of the boys. "Anything new?" He nodded toward the television and sat down in the overstuffed rocking chair he'd had delivered from his house back in Arizona.

"Not really," Colt said.

"I guess no news is good news."

Oz was set to take a massive bite from his sandwich, but he stopped and set it back down. "Mr. McAlister, I know you've done an awful lot for me . . . you know, with getting me re-instated and everything."

"I didn't do much of anything," Grandpa said. "Besides, it wasn't like you did anything wrong."

"Still, thanks," Oz said. He paused a long moment, his eyes distant as though he was recalling a forgotten memory. "It's just that I was hoping you could help me with one more thing."

"What is it, son?"

"I want to see my father."

:: CHAPTER 27 ::

Murdoch McAlister had the personal cell phone number of the president of the United States of America, but even he had his limitations. He placed calls to key contacts inside the military, including Major General Robert T. Walker, the commander in chief of the Special Operations Command, but the best he could do was arrange for a hologram communication exchange.

"Are you sure about this?" Colt said as he watched the camera operator run through a test for the HCE.

"Yeah," Oz said. "I need to talk to him one last time in case . . . well, in case something happens to me."

"Nothing is going to happen," Colt said, surprised by the anger that welled inside his chest. He wasn't mad at Oz for saying it, because it was true. None of them was promised tomorrow, but it was easier when he wasn't thinking about it.

Oz shrugged. "If you say so."

"We're all set." The camera operator opened the door to the control room and took a seat behind a panel with more levers, buttons, and dials than an air traffic control facility.

"Look, are you sure you don't want some privacy?" Colt said. He was feeling a bit squeamish—not because Santiago Romero had tried to kill him, but because he felt like a voyeur.

"You're good," Oz said. "Besides, I'm not sure I can do this alone."

That struck Colt as strange. Oz was the perfect human specimen who was willing to go hand-to-hand with one of the Thule, but he was scared to talk to his own dad by himself?

"All right, here we go," the camera operator said through a microphone.

The air shimmered, and suddenly Santiago Romero was there in the room, fully dimensional save for the fact that he was slightly transparent.

Lobo, as he was often called, was tall like Oz, but he had a bit of a paunch and he wasn't as muscular. His shoulders were hunched and his dark skin looked almost sallow, but Colt could still see the arrogance in his eyes.

He was in a solitary confinement holding cell at Fort Leavenworth for an act of treason against all of humanity—all because he had been paranoid that the government was going to remove him from his role as director of CHAOS. He had conspired with a Thule assassin to kill the deputy director of the CIA's National Clandestine Service, a federal judge, the director of the CHAOS Military Academy, and two United States senators.

"Technology is an amazing thing, isn't it?" Lobo said. "I mean, here I am locked away, and you're . . . Where are you?"

"It doesn't matter," Oz said, his eyes fixed on the floor instead of on his father.

"How have you been, son?"

"Don't do that." Oz shook his head. "Don't act like everything is fine between us, because it isn't."

Lobo sighed. "I understand that you're upset, but—"

"You don't understand anything," Oz said. "Forget what you put me through . . . that you humiliated me and that they kicked me out of the academy. What about Mom? What about all the people you had murdered? And their families? And for what? A stupid job."

"I did it for you."

"You what?" Oz stood there slack-jawed, his eyes brimming with tears. "You're kidding, right? You did it for yourself."

"Why are you here, son? To taunt me? Or did someone put you up to this?"

"No one put me up to anything! And I'm not your son. Not anymore."

"You must be enjoying this," Lobo said, turning to Colt.

"No, sir."

"Leave him out of this."

"I tried to," Lobo said. "I told them that their plan was insane—that it was *treasonous* to send children against the Thule—but they wouldn't listen to reason." Lobo curled his lip, seemed to grow stronger as he spewed his anger. "And yet I'm the one who is locked up."

A familiar rage whispered at the back of Colt's skull, and for a moment he savored the thought of snapping Romero's neck. But he pushed it away. "I forgive you," Colt said, his voice barely a whisper.

Lobo stepped back as if struck. "What?"

Colt stood up and walked over to Oz. "Even though you tried to kill me, I forgive you."

"How touching."

"I hate what you did," Oz said as he wiped his nose with the back of his sleeve. "I hate that you're a murderer—that you destroyed so many families and that you actually think you did it for me. But that's between you and God." He took a deep breath and exhaled slowly. "And even though you don't deserve it, I came here to tell you that I forgive you too."

:: CHAPTER 28 ::

I realize most of you wish you were at lunch, but can anyone
tell me what this is?" Agent Rhane held up a metal object
about the size of a Rubik's Cube. He was standing in the middle of Hologram Room 3 with members of Phantom, Jackal,
and Blizzard Squads, and he didn't look happy.

"Come on now," he said, his one good eye scanning the
crowd. "McAlister? Romero?"

Agent O'Keefe shook his head as he watched them through
the glass wall of the command center overhead. "Will one of you
numbskulls answer the man?" he said through the loudspeaker.
"You're not only embarrassing yourselves, you're embarrassing
the entire academy."

Jonas raised his hand sheepishly.

"Now how did I know you'd be the one to answer," Rhane
said. "All right, Cadet Hickman. Go ahead."

"I believe it's called a portal cube, sir."

"You sure about that?" Rhane glared at Jonas, who turned his attention to a spot on the floor near his shoes.

"Yes, sir."

"Good, because you're right," Rhane said, breaking into a rare smile. "This little doohickey is indeed called a portal cube, and it happens to be one of the most powerful bits of technology this world has ever seen. All you have to do is enter the coordinates of the place you'd like to end up and it'll open a sixty-second portal."

"Does that include the girls' dorms?" Pierce asked, earning laughter from the guys and eye rolling from the girls.

"That's about enough of you, Bowen," O'Keefe said. "One more wisecrack and you're on toilet detail."

"Shutting up now, sir," Pierce said with a melodramatic salute.

"I swear, if the Thule don't get me first, that boy will be the death of me," O'Keefe said, not realizing his microphone was still on.

"Each squad assigned to Project Betrayal will have one of these, so I want squad leaders thinking about who you would trust with your lives—because if you lose it, there's a good chance you'll be stuck on Gathmara forever. And let me tell you, it's not exactly a vacation destination—especially for humans."

"You're in charge of ours," Colt said, leaning over and whispering in Danielle's ear.

"Why me?"

"Because I trust you with my life," Colt said. "And because if I gave it to Oz, he'd either lose it or break it."

"I heard that," Oz said, nudging Colt with his elbow.

"I know."

"Show map," Rhane said, and a holomap of Dresh, the Thule capital, appeared. "This is the reactor facility," he said, tapping a domed building that sat next to the shore of a massive body of water. "And it's where we're going to spend most of our time training today."

He went on and explained how drones and soldiers from the Defense Corps, Vril, and the Dagon Alliance patrolled the facility.

"Why don't we just open up a portal and drop a nuke on 'em?" Pierce said without bothering to raise his hand.

"Because this mission is about stealth, not might," Rhane said. "Besides, a nuclear bomb wouldn't so much as crack the exterior wall of the facility. This mission has to be handled from the inside out."

CHAPTER 29

There was a rare break in the schedule before dinner the next night, so Phantom Squad decided to meet in the Agricultural Records Room to discuss everything they had learned over the past few days.

"Can you believe it? We're actually full-fledged CHAOS agents," Grey said, looking at his new uniform in the mirror.

"Junior agents," Oz said. "And for the record, it's technically the Department of Alien Affairs now, not CHAOS. The agencies were officially merged, remember? CHAOS doesn't exist."

"Let him have his moment," Danielle said, slapping Oz on the shoulder. "Besides, it isn't the Phantom Flyer and his Agents of the Department of Alien Affairs. They're still calling it the Agents of CHAOS."

"You realize that's just for show, right?" Oz said.

"Does that mean your reinstatement into the academy was just for show too?" Danielle asked.

"Not the same thing."

"Would you two knock it off?" Colt said.

"Agreed," Stacy said. "It's kind of nauseating."

Colt had been watching Danielle and Oz bicker, prod, tease, and pretend to be annoyed with each other for the better part of an hour. *Just tell each other,* he wanted to yell. *Tell each other how you really feel, because who knows how much time we have left?* Not that he was the shining example of putting himself out there. Sure, it seemed like he and Lily were at least kind of a thing, but then again, were they?

Then there was Stacy, who was sitting right next to him. She wasn't a classic beauty like Lily, but she was still attractive. And she knew as much about comic books as he did. Check that. More. But maybe Danielle was right. Maybe he liked her because it made Pierce jealous. Or maybe he just liked her. Even Stacy thought that he should go for it with Lily, but did she mean it?

"This is driving me crazy!" Danielle shouted at her computer screen.

"Need some help?" Oz said.

"Yeah," Danielle said. "What can you tell me about the Casmir effect? Or how about exotic matter and negative energy density? Know much about gravitational singularities? Cosmic strings? Quantum physics?"

Oz shrugged. "A little."

"Seriously?" Jonas asked, his mouth agape as he stared at Oz. "That's amazing. I had no idea you were interested in theoretical science."

"He isn't, so ignore him," Danielle said, turning back to her computer screen. "He's just a distraction."

"Really? You think I'm a distraction?" Oz smiled as he raised a single eyebrow. "Not that I can blame you. I mean, with these dimples? You're only human, right?"

"I'm going to need a barf bag," Danielle said.

"Oh my, are you ill?" Glyph asked. "Perhaps you should lie down. There's a terrible virus going around."

"It's a figure of speech," Danielle said. "You know . . . because he's annoying."

Glyph frowned. "No, I'm afraid I don't know."

"Never mind," she said with a sigh. "Look, I know this is going to sound rude—and I'm sorry about that—"

"Then why say it?" Oz asked, mischief dancing in his eyes.

"Seriously?" Danielle said as she spun around to glare at him, but the smile never left his face. She sighed and shook her head. "We need to focus on finding the gateway, so if you're not here to help, maybe you should find something else to do."

"About that . . . ," Jonas said, his cheeks flushing red as he stared at the floor.

"I wasn't talking about you," Danielle said.

Jonas went to put his hands in his pockets, but since cadet uniforms didn't have pockets, his hands slid down his thighs. His face turned an even deeper shade of red as he pushed his glasses up off the end of his round nose. "Look, I probably should have said something earlier, but we got a package from a courier this morning."

"A courier?" Oz said. "Like those guys on the bikes with the little bells on the handlebars?"

"Sometimes I wonder how you made it past second grade," Danielle said.

"Charm."

She rolled her eyes.

"He was actually riding an armored ultralight." Jonas unzipped the top of his backpack and pulled out a large manila envelope.

"What is it?" Danielle asked.

"Coordinates."

"From the Tesla Society?"

Jonas nodded.

"Why didn't you say anything?" Danielle asked, looking both tired and frustrated at the same time.

"It's just that Stacy told me you were still asleep, and I know you haven't been sleeping much lately, so I told her not to wake you up."

Danielle turned to Stacy. "You knew about this?"

"Don't look at me," Stacy said. "I didn't know what he wanted. And even if I had, I wouldn't have told you. He's right. You need sleep."

"Am I the only one who realizes that we're all going to die if we don't find a way to shut down the gateway?" Danielle asked as she ran her hand over her head and tugged at her ponytail.

"You're not serious, right?" Oz said.

"Yes, I'm serious!"

"Come on, Danielle," Colt said.

"Somebody has to take this seriously."

"What do you think we've been doing the last two months?" Oz said. "I mean, while you were sleeping I ran ten miles, went to the gym and lifted, took an hour of target practice, and then ran through a simulated combat session with Lohr—all before breakfast."

"Guys, stop," Colt said.

"The only reason I was sleeping is because I was up until three in the morning trying to fix the particle analyzer that you broke."

"Who cares about measuring the wind?"

"We aren't measuring the wind," Danielle said, her face bright red. She jumped out of her chair and stood in front of Oz, fists clenched at her sides. "It uses photon correlation spectroscopy to analyze anomalies in the atmosphere—as in detecting the submicron particles that are the precursors to portal formation."

Oz crossed his arms over his chest as he looked down at her. "Did you know that your nostrils flare when you're angry? It's kinda cute."

Danielle opened her mouth, then closed it again. It was the first time in recent memory that Colt had seen her at a loss for words, and he was doing his best to keep from laughing.

"This is my fault," Jonas said, his soft voice filling the silence. "I know I should have told you, but I think I found the coordinates for the gateway."

"Seriously?" Danielle asked, suddenly able to speak again. "Show me."

Jonas pulled out his tablet and opened a spreadsheet that was filled with what looked like a series of random numbers. "Okay, these two columns are the longitude and latitude of all known portals that have been reported since the inception of the CHAOS program in June of 1938. And these columns? They're soft spots. You know, where the lining that separates our atmosphere from the atmosphere of another world has started to deteriorate."

"We're not stupid," Oz said.

"Sorry."

"Stop apologizing. He's just trying to get under your skin," Danielle said, her eyes never leaving the monitor. "Can we map it?"

"Way ahead of you." Jonas entered a series of commands, and a moment later they were all looking at a map that was buried beneath thousands of dots. "The portals are green and soft spots are blue."

Danielle's eyes flitted back and forth, up and down. "I don't get it," she said. "I thought there was a pattern."

"There is," Jonas said. "Watch." He entered another series of commands, and red dots started to appear all across the map.

"What are those supposed to be?" Oz asked.

"Neutronic castoffs from actual portals."

"You mean randoms?"

Jonas frowned, looking at Oz as though he was surprised. "Exactly," he said.

Oz smiled. "I'm smarter than I look," he said as he slapped Jonas on the back with enough force that his glasses nearly fell off of his face.

"I still don't see a pattern," Danielle said.

"Here, I'll zoom in." Jonas touched the screen with his thumb and index finger pinched together, and as he spread them apart the camera zoomed in. He did it two more times until the state of West Virginia filled the entire screen, then again until they were looking at a town called Sanctuary.

All of a sudden Colt's head started to pound. It felt as though something was trying to escape his thoughts—something alien. Something Thule.

"I see the cluster. Is that a ring or something?" Danielle said, squinting as she moved until her nose was almost touching the screen.

"Watch this." Jonas hit the Enter key, and lines started to appear between the red dots until it formed what looked like a three-dimensional hourglass lying on its side.

"Regression analysis," Danielle said, as though she suddenly understood. "You found a pattern inside the subset. That's amazing!" Without warning she turned and wrapped her arms around Jonas and kissed him on the cheek.

"Yeah," Jonas said, his shoulders scrunched and his face puckered as though getting a kiss from Danielle was something akin to being kissed by a rotting zombie corpse.

"What's wrong?" Oz said. "You're, like, a hero. You found the gateway, which means we can stop the Thule. And one of the hottest girls on campus just kissed you. Are you sick or something?"

"One of?" Danielle asked, a single eyebrow raised.

For the first time that Colt could remember, Oz blushed. "Um . . . you know. I'm just saying."

"What *exactly* are you saying?" Danielle said with overemphasis.

"Later," Colt said. "Did you tell anyone that the portal opens there, in a Podunk town in West Virginia?"

Jonas lowered his eyes and shook his head slowly. "I . . . I can't."

"Why?"

"Because that Podunk town is my home."

:: CHAPTER 30 ::

I'm sorry, but we have to call this in," Colt said. He could tell something was wrong, but it didn't make sense. Jonas was just sitting there with narrowed eyes. His neck was flushed and his fists were clenched like he was angry . . . but why? If he'd actually pinpointed the exact coordinates of the gateway, then there was a chance they could shut it down before the Thule had a chance to open it.

"Spill it," Oz said.

"Leave him alone," Danielle said. "Can't you see he's upset?"

"He's hiding something."

"No, he's not."

Jonas looked at Danielle and then Oz, his eyes brimming with tears behind his glasses. "Yes, I am." His voice was weak, barely a whisper as the words spilled from quivering lips. "Nobody is supposed to know about it—not the military. Not even the president."

"What are you talking about?" Colt asked.

"That was the deal," Jonas said.

"You're not making any sense," Oz said.

Jonas ran his fingers through his hair and pulled until he grimaced under the pain. "Please don't make me do this."

"Do what?" Danielle said, her voice gentle as she placed her hand on his forearm. "Jonas, listen to me. We at least have to tell Colt's grandfather."

"No."

"What deal?" Colt said. "Why wouldn't the president know about your hometown?"

"It's complicated."

"That's not good enough," Colt said.

Jonas shook his head.

"Tell me now, or I'm calling this in."

"No!" Jonas jumped out of his chair and took Colt by the forearm.

Colt winced. He looked up and saw Jonas snarling. Had his eyes always been gold? Wait. Were his teeth pointed? Colt blinked once and again, wondering if he was losing his mind or if the medication Dr. Roth had given him was making him hallucinate. Was Jonas a Thule? No. That was impossible. Everyone on campus had to take a daily blood test to prove that they were human.

"Sorry," Jonas said, letting go. The contorted rage was replaced by contrition. Embarrassment. Shame. "It's just that . . ."

"We get it," Oz said. "Your dad is in some kind of witness protection program or something, but you know what? I don't care, because I'm not going to sit back and do nothing while an army of angry six-armed aliens is getting ready to break through and eat our livers."

"You don't understand."

"You're right, I don't." Oz glared at Jonas, his chest heaving.

"Oz, please," Danielle said, but Beauty couldn't stave off the Beast.

"For someone with an IQ that's off the charts, you're acting like an idiot," Oz said.

"Wait a minute." Everyone turned to look at Ethan, who was studying a holomap that was hovering over a metal disc in the middle of the room. "This is it, right? Your hometown?"

Jonas nodded but didn't say anything.

"It's the place where the military blocks transmissions so they can test stuff," Ethan said.

"Yes," Glyph said, his eyes lighting up. "It's the exact coordinates of the United States National Radio Quiet Zone."

"Is your dad some kind of super scientist who works for the government?" Grey asked. "You know, like Leonard Nimoy?"

"I believe Cadet Arnold meant to say Nikkola Tesla," Glyph said. "Leonard Nimoy is an American actor, film director, poet, musician, and—"

"We get it, Wikipedia," Oz said, cutting him off. "He was on some boring science fiction show. Whatever. Can we get back to the whole gateway thing?"

"Help us understand," Danielle said. "Is the Radio Quiet Zone supposed to be a secret?"

Jonas sighed. "Not exactly."

"Then you know that if you're right—if the gateway opens up in your hometown—it's going to trigger what amounts to nuclear fission," Danielle said. "And the entire state of West Virginia is going to get ripped open like a Christmas present. There won't be anything left."

Jonas closed his eyes for a moment, then opened them and looked at Colt. "I'll make you a deal," he said. "Let me go there and verify the data. If their readings match the report, then I'll make the call myself."

"And what are we supposed to do in the meantime? Sit around and wait?" Oz said. "What if the Thule open the gateway before you get there?"

"For all we know, the data could be off," Jonas said, his chin up and shoulders back as he stood in front of Oz. "Someone . . . well, something could have infiltrated the Tesla Society and planted false data."

"Why would they do that?" Oz said.

"To divert us from the real gateway," Danielle said.

"Wait, you're on his side?"

"It makes sense," Danielle said. "If we call it in and we're wrong, they'll never believe us again."

"They don't believe you now." Oz turned to Colt. "It's your call, but if you ask me, we should call it in."

"Please," Jonas said. "Give me twenty-four hours. That's all I'm asking."

What about our patrol, Squad Leader Colt McAlister?" Glyph said. "We're supposed to be in Strasburg at precisely 1930, and if I get court-martialed for defying orders, my parents will send me to the work camps on the third moon of—"

"Relax," Colt said. "We'll stop in Strasburg, and if we find anything, Bravo Team can stay behind while we head to Sanctuary."

"I could go by myself," Jonas said.

"No way," Oz said. "Too dangerous."

"He's hiding something," Pierce said. "Why else would he want to sneak away?"

"Leave him alone," Danielle said.

"Look at the way he's sweating," Pierce said. "It's obvious. He's totally hiding something."

"Did you ever think he might be sweating because we're staring at him?"

"It's more than that, isn't it, Hickman?" Pierce glared at Jonas, who turned away without saying a word. "That's what I thought."

As much as he hated to admit it, Colt had a feeling that Pierce was right. Jonas was hiding something. But if Jonas and Danielle had pinpointed the coordinates for the Thule gateway, then there was a chance they could shut it down before the Thule launched their full-scale invasion.

"I'm not trying to sneak away," Jonas said, his shoulders slumped as he stared at the ground. "It's just that . . ."

"What?" Colt asked.

"Nothing," Jonas said, though he was clearly frustrated. "Can we at least take a van instead of the Humvees? I don't want the people of Sanctuary to think they're under attack."

||||||||||||||||||||||||||||||||

They decided to stick to the back roads where they could avoid the tangled mess of freeways in and around Washington as tens of thousands fled the nation's capital.

Even the small towns were deserted. Cars had been abandoned along the side of the road, and the lights were off in all the homes. They passed a pharmacy where a sign had been posted letting everyone know that the entire inventory had been donated to the Red Cross, and someone had spray-painted a skull and crossbones and the words KILL THEM ALL across a school bus. The skull looked like an alien.

"Ignore it, Glyph," Colt said. "They're just scared, that's all."

They arrived at Strasburg twenty minutes early. Save for a few stubborn souls, the town was deserted like everywhere else. Colt offered to sweep through the surrounding area to make

DOMINATION

sure there weren't any Thule, but the sheriff said that he had it covered, so they continued on to Sanctuary.

The drive took another four hours, leaving Colt ample time to come up with a good excuse as to why he had decided to stray from his orders. The only problem was that he couldn't think of anything that sounded remotely believable.

"What if Glyph is right?" he said to Danielle. "What if they court-martial us?"

"For saving the world? I don't think so," she said. "Besides, you're the new Phantom Flyer, remember? I doubt they're going to court-martial the nation's first official superhero."

A couple of hours later they spotted a convenience store that was still open to the public, and even though they didn't need to fill up with gas, Colt decided to pull over. It had been weeks since any of them had tasted soda, potato chips, or candy bars, and they loaded up to make up for lost time.

"This is truly fascinating," Glyph said as he sniffed an open bottle of Orange Crush.

"Taste it," Danielle said.

Glyph licked the rim and smacked his lips. "It's quite sweet."

"You have to chug it to get the whole effect," Grey said.

"Yeah, like this," Oz added before downing an entire bottle of Dr Pepper. When he was done, he smiled and released an outrageously loud belch as everyone laughed.

"I don't understand," Glyph said.

"Just drink it already," Pierce said.

Glyph brought the bottle to his lips and tilted it back, downing the contents in three gulps. He blinked several times and then his eyes shot wide and he grabbed at his throat.

"What's wrong with him?" Ethan said. "Is he dying or something?"

"Someone give him the Heimlich," Grey said.

"Don't look at me," Pierce said and casually popped a Funyun into his mouth and licked his fingertips.

"Do something," Danielle said as she grabbed Colt's arm.

He was about to ask her what she wanted him to do when Glyph released the loudest and longest burp he had ever heard. When he was done, Glyph licked his lips and looked inside his empty bottle. "Do you think I could have another?"

It was closing in on ten o'clock by the time everyone loaded back into the van, and almost midnight when Colt saw the sign that welcomed them to Sanctuary, West Virginia, population 4,327.

"Pull over here," Jonas said as they approached a billboard for the Blue Moon Diner, home of Ethel's World-Famous Apple Cobbler.

"Where?" Colt asked.

"Anywhere. Just cut the lights so nobody sees us."

Gravel crunched beneath the tires as Colt eased onto the shoulder and parked the van under the billboard. "Is this hidden enough, or should we cut down some branches and cover it up?"

"It won't matter," Jonas said as he slid the door open. "They already know we're here."

"How?" Pierce said. "Do they have a satellite pointed at us or something?"

"They just know." Jonas climbed over a wooden fence and started walking across an empty field toward a line of trees.

"Where are you going?" Danielle asked, but he didn't answer.

"I always wanted to live in the country. It's so peaceful." Stacy smiled as she looked up at the stars shining brightly in the sky overhead. It was the first clear night in weeks, and Colt watched as a cool breeze whipped through her ponytail.

"I don't know about the rest of you, but I'm following Hickman," Pierce said as he shouldered his assault rifle and climbed the fence.

As they crossed the field, Colt picked up the scent of fear that Pierce kept masked under layers of arrogance and anger. It made him unstable. Unpredictable. Dangerous.

"Did you see that?" Ethan asked.

"See what?" Oz said.

"Up ahead in the tree." Ethan stopped and lifted his assault rifle to his shoulder.

"Easy," Oz said. "It's probably Hickman."

"There it is again, up in the branches!"

"Whatever you do, don't—"

A loud bang echoed through the darkness as Ethan fired his weapon.

"What are you doing?" Oz ripped the rifle out of Ethan's hand.

"Shooting an alien."

"If they didn't know we were here before, they do now," Colt said.

They pressed forward, following Jonas into the trees as a gust of wind stirred up remnants of dead leaves left over from autumn. Colt stood with feet firmly planted, his eyes scanning the darkness as the hair on the back of his neck stood on end.

CHAPTER 32

They found Jonas in an open pasture with his eyes locked on the particle analyzer that looked a lot like a smartphone. Wind swirled, blowing a light dusting of snow around them.

"How long is this going to take?" Colt asked as he looked at the clock in his heads-up display. It was fast approaching one in the morning.

"Let me talk to him, okay?" Danielle said. She walked across the frozen grass with a slow, steady pace as though she were approaching someone with a hundred sticks of dynamite taped to his chest.

"I wondered if it was going to work in the cold," Colt heard her say.

"It should work up to negative thirty-five centigrade," Jonas said, though he didn't bother to turn around and look at her.

"Wow. That's amazing."

"You don't have to pretend you're my friend," he said. "Trust me, I'm used to it."

"What are you talking about?"

"I know everyone thinks I'm a freak—that I have something to hide."

"But I *am* your friend," Danielle said. "We all are." She hesitated, as though weighing her words before she spoke them. "Look, I'm not going to say that you haven't been acting a little strange since you told us about Sanctuary—and yeah, I wish you would have told me about the new data. But that doesn't mean I think you're a freak. You're just under a lot of stress."

"You don't know the half of it."

"You could tell me," she said.

Jonas turned and stared at her.

"I mean, only if you think it would help," she said. "It's no big deal."

"There's a reason Sanctuary has been a secret for so long," Jonas said. "And trust me, if you guys knew the truth, you wouldn't want to be my friends."

"Whatever it is, I'm sure you didn't have anything to do with it."

"I wish that were true."

"Everything okay?" Colt asked as Oz loomed behind them with the .50-caliber machine gun resting across his shoulder.

Danielle nodded. "Yeah, we're fine."

"How much longer?"

She sighed and turned back to Jonas. "Well?"

"I'm done."

"And?"

"They were right. This is where the gateway is going to open. Right here on my grandpa's farm."

"That's great," Danielle said as Jonas looked at her with disbelief. "I mean, not that it's your grandpa's property—but that we found the gateway."

Jonas took a deep breath. "And now the whole world is going to know about Sanctuary, and it's all my fault."

She placed her hand on his shoulder. "Jonas, if we can find a way to stop it from opening up, you're going to get a Nobel Peace Prize for not only saving this town but the whole world."

He sighed. "I hope you're right."

There was a blur of motion as something dropped from a tree and landed on Ethan's back. Another silhouette fell on Grey, pulling him to the ground, and yet another jumped on Stacy, who screamed as she fell.

Oz was the first to react, dropping his gun as he ran to help her. Two more figures leapt, each of them landing nimbly on its feet and grabbing one of Oz's forearms. "Get off me!" he shouted, pulling them together so they smashed into one another.

"Thule!" Pierce yelled as more figures rushed out from the shadows. He opened fire, bursts of orange flaring from the muzzle of his assault rifle as bullets tore into tree trunks, dirt, and the figures that were attacking them.

"Watch it!" Oz yelled as a bullet ricocheted off his armor, but Pierce didn't listen. He screamed as he continued to pull the trigger as dozens of six-armed aliens surrounded Phantom Squad.

"No," Jonas said, shaking his head. "This can't be happening."

"Get your helmet on," Danielle said as she pulled the hand-gun from her hip holster and took aim at the nearest Thule.

"Wait!" Jonas grabbed her wrists and the gun discharged, tearing into the frozen ground. "You don't understand," he said. "They're just scared."

"Who?"

Colt felt a dark voice calling from within as adrenaline raged in his body. His breathing was shallow, and his skin started to itch as madness raged around him. He watched as Oz used his machine gun as a club and Glyph simply sidestepped each attack, using each Thule's momentum to misdirect it and send it to the ground. But something was off. These Thule weren't like the others he had seen. They were smaller, and he could tell from the reflection of the moonlight that some of their scales were gold and others blue. What was going on?

"Look out!" Danielle shouted.

Time seemed to slow, and Colt watched as the bullet erupted from the barrel of her gun. He could see the revolutions as it spun through air mere inches from his helmet before it caught one of the Thule in the shoulder. He turned and saw the alien as it writhed on the ground, kicking and moaning.

"Where are these things coming from?" Oz shouted.

"Doesn't matter, as long as we exterminate them," Pierce said. "You know what they say—the only good alien is a dead alien."

"I told you never to say that again," Colt said, watching for Glyph's reaction from the corner of his eye.

"Whatever."

Please, tell them to stop shooting.

It was Jonas, and somehow he was using mindspeak. *Are you a . . .* Colt couldn't even finish the sentence. Had Jonas been a Thule all this time, or had a shapeshifter killed the real Jonas and replaced him?

They aren't the enemy, they're just frightened, Jonas said.

A claw with razor talons raked across his mask, and Colt lashed out with the butt of his rifle, catching the alien on the side of the head. It fell in a motionless heap, green blood issuing from its earhole.

A swarm of Thule brought Glyph to the ground, and angry claws fought to remove his armor. One of the aliens grabbed Ethan's assault rifle and snapped it in half. Stacy was backed against a tree as three Thule closed in, their mouths agape and forked tongues licking the air.

Pierce stood over one of the Thule, his boot on its neck and the barrel of his gun pointed at its head. "You're even uglier up close than you are in pictures," Pierce said as the alien writhed, all six hands lashing against his armor.

"No!" Colt shouted.

Pierce turned his head to look at Colt, and the Thule's tail wrapped around his rifle before it ripped it out of Pierce's hands and flung it into the trees.

"I'm going to kill you!" Pierce pulled out his handgun as the alien morphed into a boy who couldn't have been much older than eight years old.

"Please, mister. Don't shoot me."

As Jonas watched, his face contorted with rage. His skin bubbled like water on a stove. Bones cracked. His eyes turned gold and his teeth became pointed. His armor broke at the seams, falling away as his chest expanded and his shoulders widened. The boy they knew was gone and all that remained was a Thule.

Jonas threw his head back and screamed, the sound echoing across the frozen landscape as he charged at Pierce. His tail undulated and his hands flexed as he raised his arms to strike. Pierce fired his gun, but the bullets bounced off Jonas's scaled hide as though they were nothing more than beanbags.

"I always knew you were a freak!"

Jonas knocked the gun from his hand and wrapped his fingers around Pierce's neck. With a cry he lifted Pierce off the ground, his eyes filled with madness as Pierce kicked and scrapped, trying to break free.

"That's just about enough of that." A tall man wearing a wide-brimmed hat and a brown jacket with a gold star stepped out from the tree line. His voice was calm, but he was carrying a shotgun with blue sparks dancing across the barrel like miniature bolts of lightning.

"I'm not going to tell you again, Jonas."

As Jonas turned to look at the man, his top lip curled back in a snarl. "But, Sheriff, he was going to kill Ezekiel."

"He didn't, though, so why don't you do as I say? Put the boy down and let's talk."

"Jonas . . . is that you?" A second man emerged from the shadows, this one short and heavyset.

"Dad?"

:: CHAPTER 33 ::

S heriff Sutherland didn't say a word as he drove through the winding country roads that led to the heart of Sanctuary, West Virginia.

According to the clock on the dashboard, it was just after 2:00 a.m. Colt sat in the back of the squad car with Danielle while a trail of sheriff's deputies followed with the rest of Phantom Squad, including Jonas, who had transformed back into his human form. He'd wanted to drive into town with his dad, but the sheriff wouldn't allow it.

Danielle's eyes were dilated, her breathing shallow, and she was biting her fingernails.

"It's going to be okay," Colt said as he reached over and took her hand, but when he saw the sheriff staring back at them in the rearview mirror, he wasn't sure.

Thud. Thud. Thud.

They drove over a bridge that spanned a wide river where the water rushed over rocks before it disappeared around the bend. Trees with naked branches sprouted from the banks, and in the distance they could see a church steeple silhouetted against the half moon. They passed an elementary school and then a park. Joe's Bait Shop. Dairy Queen. A water tower. Everything seemed so normal.

Main Street boasted a barbershop and a diner, Sears Roebuck Co., a bank, and a Sinclair station on the corner. Sheriff Sutherland parked in front of the courthouse, where a stout man in a black overcoat and matching fedora stood at the base of the steps. His cheeks were round and red, and if he'd had a white beard and mustache, he would have been the perfect Santa Claus.

"How do you do?" he said after Sheriff Sutherland opened the back door. "I hear that you're the young man in charge of this operation. Cadet McAlister, is it?"

Colt nodded.

"Excellent. I'm Martin Luther Cross, mayor of Sanctuary, and I believe you've met our fine sheriff, Orville Sutherland."

"Yes, sir." Colt accepted his hand, but he was confused by the reception. If the people of Sanctuary didn't like visitors, why was he being so kind? Was he trying to keep Colt off guard, or had Jonas overreacted?

The mayor shook his hand vigorously. "I don't mind telling you that Sanctuary doesn't get too many visitors, particularly at this time of day. But I've asked Ethel to open up the diner and make us a pot of coffee and warm up some of that homemade apple cobbler. My wife has me on a bit of a diet," he said, patting his ample belly, "but I think it might help calm our nerves. What do you say?"

"I appreciate the offer, but we need to get back," Colt said.

"Well, here's the thing about that," Mayor Cross said. He placed his arm around Colt's shoulder as though the two had known each other for years. "I'm afraid folks around here are a bit worked up. Now typically when someone stumbles upon our little town, we're able to point him in the right direction before any harm is done. But I'm afraid you and your friends have learned a bit more than what makes us comfortable, if you catch my meaning."

He started to guide Colt toward the Blue Moon Diner across the street, but when Oz tried to follow, the sheriff blocked his path.

"You don't want to do that," Oz said. "Two arms or six, I'll break 'em all just the same."

"Is that so?" Sheriff Sutherland smiled in a way that made it look like he hoped Oz would try.

"I'll be fine," Colt said to Oz. "Just make sure Pierce doesn't do anything stupid."

:: CHAPTER 34 ::

The Blue Moon Diner wasn't very big. There were six booths, three on either side, and a counter where four more people could sit, read the paper, and drink a cup of coffee with their cobbler. The Penguins were singing "Earth Angel" in the background while a woman with gray hair and horn-rimmed glasses poured coffee into two porcelain cups.

"Sit anywhere," she said as she placed the coffee back on the burner and wiped her hands on her crisp white apron.

"Thank you, Ethel," Mayor Cross said. He removed his hat and coat and looked around the room as though he was survey-ing his options. Colt wanted him to pick something in the back of the diner, away from prying eyes, but the mayor slid into the booth next to the front window. "How is this?" he said as he threw his tie over his shoulder.

"Fine, thanks." Colt felt the eyes of the townspeople boring into him as he took his seat across from the mayor. Everything had happened so fast, and now he found himself wondering if he should have listened to Oz and reported the randoms right away.

"Here you are," Ethel said as she gave each of them a cup of coffee and a heaping plate of apple cobbler. "Can I get you anything else? Maybe some vanilla ice cream to go with it?"

"That sister of yours is going to be upset enough that I'm eating the cobbler, particularly at this time of night. Or morning, whatever it is," Mayor Cross said with a wave of his hand. "I better skip the à la mode."

"What about you, young man?"

"No, thank you," Colt said.

"Well, if you need anything, just holler. I'll be in the back making biscuits."

"Will do," the mayor said, not wasting any time as he dug his fork through the crumble of brown sugar, oats, and butter and into the soft apple filling. "Wait until you taste it," he said as he chewed. "It's heaven on a plate." He took another bite and licked a crumb from his lip before he dabbed at his cheek with a napkin.

"Now," he said before taking a sip of coffee. "Let's get the hard part out of the way, shall we?"

"Sure."

"As you can see, Sanctuary isn't your average town," Mayor Cross said. "We're what you might call a social experiment. You see, the Thule of this town represent a segment of our society who believe in peace and harmony. So when our brothers joined forces with Hitler's Nazis back in the thirties, we fled Germany and settled in the United States."

"You've been living here since World War II?"

"Yes," the mayor said. "But there have been Thule on your planet for centuries." He waved his hand. "But that's not the point. What you need to know is that we're what you would call a secret society, and we protect that secrecy vigorously."

Colt stopped midbite, knowing full well that the mayor was threatening him. "We don't want to give away your secret. It's just that we think we've found the spot where the Thule plan to open their gateway."

"Yes, Jonas told me a bit about that," Mayor Cross said. "Don't get me wrong, it's fascinating, but I'm afraid he's mistaken."

"He said the tests verified his research. If the Thule are going to use Sanctuary as the launching point for their attack, there's a good chance everyone who lives here is going to die."

"So what would you have us do? Leave our homes and try to live among people who revile us? Who would rather have us dead?"

Colt could smell the sadness on the man. It was so different from the rage that he sensed with the warrior Thule. The mayor was a person just like him, or like Glyph or Lohr. Sure, he took a different shape, but it was obvious that he cared about the people he served.

"Jonas said you have a portal that leads back to Gathmara."

The mayor nodded. "We convert thermal energy from a hydroelectric power plant to keep it open. In fact, Jonas's father—Dr. Hickman—designed the plant himself."

"You need to shut it down."

The mayor stopped before he took another bite of his cobbler, his jaw slack and his brow furrowed. "Excuse me?"

"The Thule—well, the bad ones, anyway—they're going to use it to power their gateway."

"Even if that was true, I'm afraid I can't make that decision alone." Mayor Cross took a last bite of his cobbler before he dabbed at the corner of his mouth with a napkin. "The entire town will have to vote, and I don't see that happening until tonight at the earliest."

"But—"

The mayor raised his hand to cut Colt off. "The question is what to do with you and your friends between now and then." He sighed. "Now I can tell you that the sheriff will want to lock you up, but I think that might be a touch drastic, especially since there's more than enough room out at the Hickman place. As long as I have your word that you'll behave yourselves, I don't see why you couldn't stay there."

:: CHAPTER 35 ::

Mrs. Hickman was standing on the front porch when the squad cars pulled into her driveway at four in the morning. She was wearing her bathrobe and fuzzy slippers, and her hair was rolled up in curlers. She ran down the steps to greet her son.

"Mom, stop!" Jonas tried to wriggle free from her bear hug as she kissed his forehead and cheeks.

"Let me look at you," she said as she held him at arm's length. "Are you okay?"

"I'm fine."

"Where's your father?"

Jonas shrugged. "I think he went to work, but I'm not sure."

"And you're not hurt?"

"You're embarrassing me."

"Oh, pishposh," she said, waving her arms. "Now the lot of you need to get inside before you catch cold. Go on now."

She ushered them into the dining room where there was enough bacon, eggs, and pancakes for everyone to have seconds and even thirds.

"We just want to go to bed," Jonas said.

"Not until you've eaten something," Mrs. Hickman insisted. She filled each of their glasses with freshly squeezed orange juice and heaped food onto their plates. "Eat up now. All of you."

They ate in relative silence, each of them too tired to argue and too nervous to sleep, knowing that both Jonas and Mrs. Hickman were actually Thule. Colt could tell Jonas was nervous since he refused to look anybody in the eye, and Pierce spent most of the meal scowling at him from across the table.

When they were finished, Danielle started to clear the plates, but Mrs. Hickman took them out of her hands.

"Absolutely not," she said. "You're our guests. And besides, you must be exhausted after all you've been through. Jonas, why don't you give your friends a tour? We have plenty of beds if anyone wants to take a nap before the vote tonight."

"Nobody wants a tour," Jonas said.

"Go on now," Mrs. Hickman said. "Just do as I say and then you can sleep."

"Fine." Jonas rolled his eyes before he led them through the house, showing them the unfinished basement, the main living area, and the second floor, where there were three bedrooms and an office. "Sorry, but I'm not allowed to go in there," he said as he shut the door—but not before Colt spotted a plaque that declared that Dr. Zachariah Hickman was a member of the Tesla Society.

There was another flight of stairs that took them up to an

attic that had been converted into a media room, complete with a sixty-inch television, surround-sound speakers, a mini-fridge stocked with soda, an old couch, and some beanbag chairs.

"You got any video games?" Grey asked.

"Don't you want to sleep?"

Grey shrugged. "Maybe later."

"Help yourself." Jonas walked over and opened a cabinet that had row after row of titles to choose from, on three different gaming systems.

"If I had a room like this, I'd never leave my house," Grey said as he grabbed *Zombie Exterminator 3* off the shelf. "Anyone want to kill some undead?"

"I'm in!" Ethan plopped down on a beanbag chair.

Stacy shrugged. "It's not like there's anything else to do."

"We got room for one more," Grey said.

"You're kidding, right?" Pierce said. "You're going to sit around here and kill zombies while we're trapped in a town full of Thule?" He turned to Colt. "You're our squad leader. Don't you have a plan or something?"

"Take a look out the window," Colt said.

"What are you talking about?"

"Just do it."

Pierce walked over and peered through slats in the blinds. An unmarked sedan was parked on the gravel beneath a streetlamp, and even though it was partially hidden behind a tree, he could see two figures sitting inside, one with a set of binoculars and the other smoking a cigarette. "Who are they?"

"Deputies," Colt said. "They're here to make sure we don't wander off."

"So what?" Pierce said. "We can't just sit here."

"I'm open to suggestions."

"How about I get some sleep while you guys take first watch," Oz said as he stretched out on a beanbag chair.

"Danielle told me that when Koenig tried to open a gateway at the Trident Biotech facilities back in Arizona, you used a computer virus to shut it down," Jonas said. "What if I could get inside the server room at the power plant? Do you think you could do it again?"

:: CHAPTER 36 ::

They waited until after lunch to put their plan in motion.

Jonas was nervous as he drove up to the guard gate at the hydroelectric power plant, but when the security guard saw who it was, he smiled and waved him through. Getting through the front door was just as easy.

"How long are you in town for?" the guard whose nameplate read M. Kunkel asked.

"A couple of days," Jonas said. "Is my dad around?"

"As a matter of fact, I just saw him," the guard said. "He mentioned something about a meeting, but I'm not sure who it was with. Would you like me to call his assistant?"

"I bet he's in one of the conference rooms on the second floor," Jonas said, hoping that the guard wouldn't notice that his hands were shaking.

"Go on up," the guard said. "And when you see him, tell him

I haven't forgotten about those Redskins tickets that he promised. They play my Steelers next week."

"I will." Jonas walked to the elevator on the far side of the lobby and placed his hand on the biometric scanner. Green circles lit around his thumb and fingertips and the door opened, but he had no intention of going to the second floor. He pressed the button for the third floor, where they kept the server room.

His heart pounded in his chest as he walked past security guards and surveillance cameras, but nobody stopped him. The server room was at the end of a winding hall, and just as he reached into his pocket to pull out the USB drive with the virus, someone called his name.

"Jonas?"

He turned around to see his dad standing there, a confused look on his face.

"What are you doing here?"

"I . . . um . . ." Jonas had an IQ that was off the charts, but he had never been quick on his feet and he wasn't very good at lying. "I came to see you."

Dr. Hickman frowned. "My office is on the first floor."

"I know," Jonas said, fumbling over his words. "Mike. You know, the security guard? Anyway, he told me you might be up here, and he was right."

"This is a restricted area, son."

"Restricted? I've been here hundreds of times."

"Things have changed, and not for the better." Dr. Hickman was nervous as he looked up and down the hallway. "Stay close," he said as he walked toward a set of double doors. "And if anyone stops us, you let me do the talking. Understood?"

They ended up back on the first floor in Dr. Hickman's office. He pulled out a device and scanned to make sure there weren't any recording devices in the room.

"Dad—"

Dr. Hickman raised an index finger to his lips as he ran the scanner over a framed photograph of the Hickman family that hung on the wall next to his desk. He scanned his desk drawers, the bottom of his chair, and even the contents of his trash can before he finally sat down.

"Is someone bugging your office?" Jonas asked.

"Not anymore," Dr. Hickman said. "At least not that I can tell."

"Why would someone want to bug you?"

"Because they think I'm a traitor," Dr. Hickman said.

"A traitor?"

"We don't have much time, so I'm going to give you the abbreviated version," Dr. Hickman said. "The day you left for the academy, one of Koenig's agents paid Mayor Cross a visit. His message was fairly clear. Either the people of Sanctuary renounce Earth and take up arms against humanity, or after the invasion we'll all be tortured and then executed."

"What did Mayor Cross do?"

"What any politician in his place would do," Dr. Hickman said. "He promised to spread the word and report any resistance."

"Like you."

"Like me."

"What about Sheriff Sutherland?"

"Near as I can tell he's on our side," Dr. Hickman said. "But it's hard to be sure."

"Aren't you scared?" Jonas asked.

"I probably should be, but mostly I'm concerned about what's going to happen to you and your mother."

"What are you going to do?"

"I'm going to stick around here and make things as difficult for Koenig and his Defense Corps as I can." Dr. Hickman smiled. "Your turn," he said. "What are you doing here?"

Jonas explained his theory about the randoms and how he had used the theory to pinpoint the exact location where he thought that the Thule would open up their gateway. He took the USB drive out of his pocket and slid it across the desk. "It's the same virus they used to shut the portal down at the Trident Biotech facility."

"I'm impressed," Dr. Hickman said. "But I'm afraid it won't work."

"Why not?"

"Because I've already tried. Over the last three months the portal has nearly doubled in size—and that's after I cut the power supply."

"How can that be?"

"They're powering it from the other side."

:: CHAPTER 37 ::

It was almost six o'clock.

Mrs. Hickman had made them a dinner of fried chicken, mashed potatoes, gravy, homemade dinner rolls, and something called Snickers Salad, but Colt wasn't hungry. He couldn't stop thinking about what they were going to do if the town voted against shutting down their hydroelectric power plant. Violence would be unavoidable.

Now he followed Mayor Cross, Dr. Hickman, and Sheriff Sutherland onto the stage of the Sanctuary High School auditorium. The mayor was all smiles as he walked over to the rickety podium, but thanks to Jonas, Colt knew it was just an act. He was half surprised to see an American flag hanging from a brass pole next to the state flag of West Virginia instead of the red flag with Koenig's black Defense Corps symbol against a white circle.

The other members of Phantom Squad were sitting up front

as requested—supposedly as guests of the town, even though it was obvious they were sitting there so the mayor and his cronies could keep them in full view. Their armor had been confiscated along with their weapons, but Jonas, with his father's assistance, had equipped them with small earpieces that had microphones so they could remain in contact.

The residents of Sanctuary filed in until every seat from the front row to the top of the balcony was filled. The custodians even set up folding chairs along the back wall and down the aisles, but there still weren't enough seats.

According to Dr. Hickman, the town was split down the middle. One faction wanted to join Koenig's Defense Corps, and the other wanted to side with humanity and fight them. The only problem was figuring out how to tell them apart. Colt scanned the audience, but they looked like average people, not warmongering aliens.

The mayor stood there waiting for everyone to quiet down. He didn't clear his throat or even tap on the microphone. He just leaned against the podium like a farmer watching his crops grow.

Soon people nudged their neighbors and pointed to the stage, and in a few minutes it was quiet enough that Colt could hear the hum of the radiators blowing warm air into the freezing auditorium.

"That's better," Mayor Cross said as he adjusted the microphone stand that was fixed to the top of the podium. "Now, I don't need to tell you why we're here tonight."

"We're here because the federal government turned its back on us, just like I always said it would!"

"Is that you, Earl Drummond?" the mayor asked as dozens of others echoed their agreement.

"You know good and well that it is." An older man with the beginnings of a beard stood up and removed his John Deere cap. He wore blue jeans and a flannel shirt, and even though he had a bit of a paunch that hung over his belt buckle, his shoulders were wide and his chest was broad.

"What if these kids are telling the truth?" the mayor said. "Would you be able to sleep at night knowing that we could have saved millions of human lives? Or perhaps the better question is, should those lives even matter?"

A woman with blond hair pulled back in a twist stood up in the front row of the balcony. "I suppose you want us to grovel before Koenig and his thugs, is that it? Do we beg for mercy, or have you forgotten why we defected from Gathmara to begin with?"

"I merely ask the question," the mayor said, his voice pleasant and a smile on his face.

There was a commotion as a group of men pushed their way to the stage, each of them wearing a red armband with Koenig's Defense Corps symbol. "Enough talk," one said. "It's time to declare our loyalty to our people!"

"Easy now." The sheriff walked toward them with his arms held wide. "Whatever it is you boys are planning to do, you'd best think—"

The first man with the armband bounded up the stairs on the side of the stage, lowered his shoulder, and caught the sheriff in the midsection. The sheriff slid across the floor and into the podium, which fell with a bang. Feedback screeched through the speakers as the man turned and rushed at Colt. Bones cracked and skin morphed into scales as the man shape-shifted into a Thule.

Jaws wide and claws raised, it attacked. Colt caught two of its hands and fell back, bending his knees and planting his feet in the Thule's stomach. He kicked with all his strength as he rolled into a backward somersault, and the Thule flew through the air and into the orchestra pit.

As Colt rolled to his feet, a heavyset man in faded blue jeans and a thermal undershirt raised a shotgun to his shoulder and took aim at him, but Jonas jumped onto the stage and stepped between Colt and the gunman.

"We're not like them, Mr. Tasker!" Jonas said. "We're not monsters, and we don't have to resort to violence. You taught me that in seventh-grade history."

"Maybe I was wrong," the man said.

"No, you weren't." Jonas took a careful step toward him, then another. "Please, Mr. Tasker. If you do this, then everything we sacrificed for all these years will be for nothing. We can show everyone that we really are different—that when humanity needed us most, we were right there standing beside them."

"I'm sorry." Mr. Tasker's hands were shaking, and there were tears in his eyes as he pulled the trigger.

"No!" Dr. Hickman stepped in front of his son, and as buckshot that glowed blue hit him, his arms flew up and his back arched. He fell, and a bloom of green liquid spread across his crisp white shirt.

"Dad! Please, you have to get up. Please." Jonas was crying as he knelt beside his father, shaking his shoulders as he pleaded with him. "Don't do this. Don't leave me!"

Dr. Hickman pulled his hand away from the wound, and it was covered in blood. He closed his eyes and took a series of shallow breaths, but when he tried to get up he only had the strength to lift his head before he fell back to the floor. "I'm . . ." He grimaced as he started to cough. "I know it looks . . ."

"You're going to be okay," Jonas said, brushing away his tears with the back of his sleeve.

"Find . . . your mom," Dr. Hickman said, the coughing fits staining his lips with green blood. "Get . . . her . . ." He closed his eyes. "Out . . ." His head fell to the side.

Jonas was crying openly, and when he looked up he saw the barrel of the mayor's pistol pointed at his head.

"I'm sorry, son," the mayor said. "But I'm afraid you're next."

The shriek of a whistle cut through the air, distant at first but growing louder with each passing moment. The mayor's eyes grew wide and he lowered his gun just a little.

Colt took advantage of the distraction. He lashed out, hitting the mayor in the wrist, and the gun flew from his hand and skittered across the floor. The mayor's eyes flashed red, and as he snarled he revealed a set of wicked teeth meant for rending flesh from bone. For a split second Colt thought the mayor was going to morph into his native Thule form, but a missile struck and the auditorium shook.

Colt was knocked to his feet as chunks of plaster fell from the ceiling. Dust and debris clung to the air like fog. The room was a cacophony of screaming, coughing, and crying as people ran for the exits. Another missile struck, this time punching a hole in the ceiling. His ears ringing and vision blurred, Colt looked for the mayor but couldn't find him.

"Colt!" Oz grabbed him by the shoulder and spun him around. His eyes were crazed, and his face and hair were caked in dust.

"What's going on?" Colt demanded. "Who's firing missiles?"

"There're at least three Trackers outside," Oz said.

"Trackers? Did they come through the portal?"

"Heck if I know."

:: CHAPTER 38 ::

Colt slipped into the foyer, hoping to find the rest of Phantom Squad. There was more screaming as the bulbs flickered overhead like a series of cameras flashing. Sparks flared, ceiling tiles fell, and the lights went out.

It didn't take long for his eyes to adjust, but Colt didn't see anyone he recognized. "Testing," he said. "Testing 1, 2, 3. Can anybody hear me?"

There was a long string of static followed by a disjointed message that popped in and out. "Some kind of . . . I don't know . . . maybe a science lab."

"That's Danielle," Colt said as he grabbed a kid wearing a letterman's jacket. "Which way to the science labs?"

"Over there." The kid pointed back over his shoulder before he broke free and ran off.

Colt took off, with Oz close behind. It was almost seven

o'clock and the sun was long gone. So was the electricity. The only source of light came from the red glow of an EXIT sign that hung near a set of double doors. As they pushed ahead, Colt realized that he had never felt more alive. He felt as though his senses had been unleashed to their full capacity for the first time. He could smell the residue from gunpowder, sense Oz's anticipation, and suddenly he could see through the darkness as though it were fully lit.

"Which way?" Oz asked when they came to a juncture of hallways.

Colt strained to both listen and smell. He could hear a low growl emanating from the darkness up ahead, and then he saw something large moving through the shadows. Claws raked against the brick walls, sending sparks. The creature stopped to sniff the air, then cocked its head and reached for a doorknob. When the door didn't open, the creature pounded on it and it quickly shattered.

"Hurry!" Danielle shouted.

Colt and Oz raced down the hall and into the room in time to see the Thule standing over Danielle, who cowered in the corner.

Oz rushed past Colt, and the Thule lashed out with its tail and caught him in the head. He crumpled and it attacked again, this time catching him across the chest.

The faint sound of explosions played in the background. The Thule growled and moved toward Colt, battering desks before it grabbed him by the jaw. A massive scar ran over its brow ridge, across a milky cataract, and down its muzzle. Its breath was rancid, like roadkill that had been left to decay in the sun.

Its eyes narrowed as it sniffed the air. "Yes," it said. "You are the one Koenig has been searching for. You are the Betrayer."

Colt's chest heaved as adrenaline washed over him. Euphoria. Power. The crucial need to protect the people around him. He struck the Thule in its injured eye, and it staggered but didn't fall. Its tail pounded the ground, breaking the floorboards.

The Thule picked up four chairs and hurled them at Colt, who covered his face with his arms. Wood shattered upon impact, and when it was over Colt stood there, dumbfounded. He should have felt pain. He should have been knocked over. It didn't make sense.

A grotesque smile spread across the alien's lips. "My name will be praised after I kill you."

Faster than Colt could react, it reached out and took his throat with one hand while two others wrapped around his shoulders. Another tried to rake across his face, but Colt grabbed it by the wrist and twisted. There was a pop, and the Thule howled as its hand went limp.

Enraged, it hefted Colt off the ground, but Colt struck the nerve cluster under its arm, and it dropped him. It lashed out with its claws, but Colt sidestepped, grabbed a chair, and smashed it over the Thule's head. Wood splintered, and Colt rammed what was left of the chair leg through the alien's gullet. It cried out in pain as it fell.

Colt looked at Oz, lying still on the floor, and emotion washed over him. "Are you dead?" Colt asked.

Oz opened one eye. "What do you think, McAlister?"

:: CHAPTER 39 ::

olt led Oz and Danielle back down the stairs and through the foyer to a set of glass doors, where they caught up with the rest of Phantom Squad. But they all stopped short when they saw a Tracker standing in the parking lot.

Covered in what looked like reclaimed metal from German panzer tanks, it was thick and lumbering, with a gun turret in place of a head and two spotlights mounted to its chest. One arm was an actual cannon, the other a claw that it used to pick up a car and throw it at the school.

"Get down!" The wall shook and glass cracked as Colt shielded Danielle.

"That thing has to be thirty feet tall." Pierce reached as though he was going to push the door open, but Oz pulled him back.

"What are you doing?"

"I want to get a closer look," Pierce said. "Besides, it's not like it can see us. It doesn't have any eyes."

"It doesn't need eyes," Oz said. "It has sensors."

"What are those?" Grey asked as three armored vehicles with mechanical legs instead of tires skittered toward the Tracker. Soldiers manning .50-caliber machine guns mounted to the top of each vehicle opened fire on the Tracker.

"Class 1 Armored Walkers," Oz said. "But the only one I've seen was a prototype."

The Tracker tried to stomp on the nearest Walker, but the Walker was too fast. It dodged out of the way and crawled up the Tracker's leg and onto its back and then its shoulder. The other Walkers followed suit, and the Tracker lashed out in vain with its clawed hand.

Colt spotted a yellow school bus on the other side of the parking lot. "Does anybody know how to hotwire a car?" he asked.

"Is that a trick question?" Oz said. He followed Colt's gaze until he saw the bus. "You can't be serious."

"I don't see anything else big enough to carry all of us."

Oz shook his head. "Yeah, I can hotwire a bus."

"Good, because this might be our only chance." Colt burst out the door and into the parking lot, weaving between the vehicles.

"Here comes another one!" Pierce shouted.

A tremor shook the ground, and when Colt looked up he saw a second Tracker. It had an actual head with glowing eyes, and instead of a claw or a cannon it had articulated hands with five fingers. And it was heading right for them.

"Run!" Colt shouted. He could feel his heart pounding in

his chest as he jumped up on the trunk of a Toyota Camry, leapt onto the roof, and then jumped back down to the asphalt.

The bus was only a hundred yards away, but the Tracker was closing in fast.

"Hurry!" Colt shouted. He looked back over his shoulder and saw a tentacle shoot out from the Tracker's palm and lash around Pierce, hefting him off the ground. Pierce shouted, his arms and legs waving.

Oz stopped next to a fallen soldier and picked up his assault rifle.

"What are you doing?" Colt shouted. "Hotwire the bus. I'll get Pierce."

For a moment Oz hesitated, then he turned and ran as the shoulder of one of the Trackers opened. A cannon emerged, and the barrel flared to life as gunfire lit the sky, chewing up the asphalt and ripping through cars.

Colt felt power surge through his body as a flood of adrenaline raged. His chest heaved and a feeling of euphoria overtook him as the world slowed down. He ran toward the Tracker and leapt, grabbing hold of the tentacle that held Pierce. Colt pulled and metal groaned and the casing bent as it lashed back and forth, taking Colt on a dizzying ride. He squeezed harder, every fiber of every muscle straining. A second tentacle shot out and caught him on the side of the head.

"Get out of here!" Pierce yelled.

Colt let go, rolling as he hit the ground. In a series of motions he fished five magnetic grenades out of his ammo belt, set the detonators, and threw them at the juncture where the tentacles were connected to the hand of the Tracker. There was a short delay before the explosions, then the tentacle released Pierce before it fell away. He dropped to the ground, landing awkwardly and rolling his ankle.

"Hey! Over here!" Colt waved his arms up and down.

"What are you doing?" Pierce asked.

"It's called a distraction—now go!"

"I can't get up!"

"Go!"

Pierce forced himself to his feet, half limping and half running toward the bus.

The Tracker stepped toward Colt and the ground shook. Its head swiveled as it reached out a massive hand. Tentacles coiled around Colt's shoulders, pinning his arms to his chest as it turned and headed for the football field.

Colt fought against the bonds, but despite his strength he couldn't break free. The Tracker deposited him in the middle of the football field where five Thule transport ships were docked.

Thule warriors with massive guns stood watch over at least two dozen prisoners, including Sheriff Sutherland. There were too many Thule to try to escape, so Colt made his way to the sheriff to see if he could get any information.

"What happened?" he asked.

"To tell you the truth, I'm not sure," the sheriff said. "Near as I can tell, the mayor must have coordinated the strike with Koenig, and we lost."

"Now what?"

"They take us back to Gathmara where we'll be declared traitors. Then, depending on Koenig's mood, we'll either be sent to labor camps or executed."

CHAPTER 40

C olt was separated from the other prisoners and placed in a holding cell that had no light. The stench of metal, gasoline, and burning oil made his stomach churn, and the cacophony of sound echoing off the walls made it impossible to orient himself.

He felt the engines rumble to life, and moments later the transport lifted off the ground. Panic fought to take hold, but Colt clung to the words that had become so familiar. *God is our refuge and strength, a very present help in trouble.*

He breathed in through his nose and out through his mouth as he waited for his eyes to adjust, but his enhanced night vision didn't give him much of an advantage. *This is where I'm supposed to be*, he reminded himself. He was in a room that wasn't much bigger than a closet, and as far as he could tell the closest thing to a door was a small vent about the size of a license plate. Not that it mattered. If he found a way to escape, it wasn't like he could fly.

"Hello! Is anybody there? Anybody?"

The dull thud of footsteps was accompanied by muffled voices, but whatever language they were speaking, it wasn't English. The footsteps stopped, and suddenly the wall behind him opened up. Colt felt a burst of pain as someone drove a needle through his neck. He spun around to see who was there, but his knees buckled and he fell.

He felt dizzy. Nauseated. And as he looked up he saw the silhouettes of two hulking figures standing against the bright light.

"Is that him?"

"The one they believe is the Betrayer? Yes. Yes, it is."

The voice was deep and horrible, and Colt saw a long, lizard-like tongue slip out from the speaker's lips as though it was tasting the air.

"He's still wrapped in human flesh," the second figure said. Through his blurred vision, Colt could see rich green scales, a yellow-green underbelly, and scar tissue running along its neck and shoulder and across one of its thighs.

"Where are we?" Colt was slipping into darkness. His own words sounded strange in his ears, like he was somehow speaking in slow motion. His lips felt numb and rubbery, and he could no longer feel his tongue.

Strange thoughts filled his mind as he shut his eyes. Buildings burning. People screaming. His grandfather, young again, but he was lying dead in the middle of a battlefield as German soldiers rolled past his corpse in panzer tanks. Danielle running as Thule gave chase.

"Sleep," one of the Thule said as everything went black.

:: CHAPTER 41 ::

Colt woke up in a fog, his head pounding and throat parched as the ground shook, tilting first to the right and then the left. He cracked his eyes open, and from what he could see he was in some kind of holding cell with a single bulb that was caged by wire.

His arms were bound behind his back as he sat cross-legged on the floor, and his neck was constrained by a collar that was bolted to the wall. He tested the length of the chain, but there wasn't much give.

The room echoed with the roar of an engine, but it wasn't until someone moaned that Colt realized he wasn't alone. The walls of the cell were lined with prisoners, each bound as he was, though none was awake. He shook his head, desperate to clear his vision as the effects of whatever the Thule had drugged him with started to wear off.

The room shook as he looked in vain for a familiar face, all the while hoping that Danielle, Oz, and the others had managed to get away. Or maybe they were dead. Either way, Colt had to push those thoughts to the back of his mind so he could concentrate on escaping.

The hot air was thick with moisture, and his entire body was coated in sweat. He wondered if his wrists were slick enough to slip though the cuffs, but the metal bracelets were too tight. He tried to snap the chain that held them together, but it refused to break. Exhausted, he closed his eyes and laid his head against the wall, trying not to give in to despair.

It wasn't long before he heard the sound of feet shuffling and keys rattling, and when the door finally opened, Colt saw the man behind all his misery.

Still fighting your destiny? Aldrich Koenig walked over and put a hand beneath Colt's collar so he could pull him to his feet. "It's time," he said, this time aloud.

"What are you going to do to me?"

Koenig smiled. "Take you back to Gathmara where you'll be publicly executed, proving once and for all that we are mightier than the superstitions of our forefathers. The Betrayer will die, and I will take my rightful place as the head of the five armies. Once we're united I'll come back to Earth and exterminate all of humanity." He licked his lips. "Though perhaps I will spare your Lily to be my bride. She is, after all, a rare beauty."

Raw fury leapt inside of Colt as he fought to break free from his restraints.

Koenig simply smiled. "Oh yes . . . a rare beauty."

Colt closed his eyes and imagined the massive gateway

swirling in the atmosphere over Sanctuary. He pictured massive airships emerging from the portal, accompanied by a fleet of Taipan star fighters.

Yes, something like that, Koenig said.

It felt disgusting, but Colt concentrated as he painted the picture in his mind. The air shimmered and then it shook. The gateway started to expand until a flash of light burst and the portal disappeared. The airships were engulfed in the blast, and as they fell from the sky, it was Colt's turn to smile.

Koenig slammed Colt against the wall, and the air exploded from his lungs.

"They'll . . . find me," Colt said.

"No, they won't," Koenig said with a sneer. As he turned and left, Colt broke into a wide smile. Koenig had invaded his thoughts, but Colt had managed to steal a thought of his own. It was only for a split second, but Colt knew what they had to do. Koenig had let slip an image of the reactor that powered the gateway, and all Colt had to do was find it.

:: CHAPTER 42 ::

We weren't always like that," Sheriff Sutherland said, his voice echoing out of the darkness.

Colt squinted and caught the silhouette of the man shackled to the wall. As his eyes adjusted, other shapes started to take form, most of them citizens of Sanctuary. All of them shackled.

"Where are they taking us?"

The sheriff coughed, rattling his chains as he turned toward Colt. "We're meant to be examples. Koenig wanted one Betrayer—apparently you—but he found himself a whole village of traitors. He'll execute the adults and turn the children into slaves." He coughed again. "It would have been better for them to die. At least then their souls would be spared."

Souls? Colt had never stopped to consider what the Thule believed, but he remembered seeing the church steeple as it towered over Sanctuary. Had the Thule brought their faith with them, or had they discovered God on Earth?

"What can you tell me about the Betrayer?" Colt said.

There was a soft thud as the sheriff leaned his head against the wall.

"To understand the Betrayer, you need to understand Gathmara." He coughed some more. "You've seen pictures, haven't you?"

Colt nodded.

"Steel cities. Poisonous clouds. Sludge-choked seas. But it wasn't always like that," Sheriff Sutherland said. "When I was young the five warlords who ruled our land were at peace for the first time in generations. There were sparkling rivers and pristine forests. We'd swim in the water and then climb up to the top of the trees and soak in the sun. And the music? That's what I remember most. One family would start the singing at sunset, and you'd hear it up and down along the river until the stars were high."

The sheriff sighed. "But it's gone, and I'm sorry to say that there are only a few of us old enough to remember it." He paused, staring off into nothing. "But when I walk by one of the parks and watch our children at play, I know that Gathmara is still alive in their spirit."

"What happened?" Colt asked.

"Aldrich Koenig." Sheriff Sutherland shook his head as his words turned sour. "Though he was born into poverty, he had great ambition. He joined the militia when he was eleven or twelve, and it wasn't long before he earned the favor of Arcos, warlord of the Defense Corps. Koenig used his cunning to manipulate Arcos into breaking the peace, promising that he would ensure that the other warlords would bow before Arcos and pay him tribute.

"It resulted in genocide. Koenig created a special unit of elite killers, and tens of thousands were slaughtered in his name. Once the Defense Corps had dominion over the five armies, Koenig turned his attention to commerce. He ushered in our modern age with his factories, and the Undarians, the people of the seas, took umbrage with the pollution, and when agreement could not be met, they declared war.

"With the blessing of Arcos, Koenig led the unified forces of the five armies against the Undarians, and when they were victorious he urged Arcos to declare Thule supremacy over all of Gathmara. And when that was accomplished, they turned their eyes to neighboring worlds. Koenig claimed that they could be harboring the Betrayer, and if the Thule didn't destroy them, they would surely destroy the Thule.

"About that time Arcos grew sick, and since he had no heir he declared Koenig warlord of the Defense Corps. The singing stopped. The children stopped playing in the rivers. Every able-bodied Thule was put to work under the auspices that we were living under an imminent threat. Fear drove us to slave in Koenig's factories, building weapons of war while his wealth grew beyond compare."

"Why didn't someone assassinate him?" Colt asked.

"It wasn't for lack of desire," the sheriff said. "There were several attempts, but they all failed. Koenig isn't a very trusting man, and if you weren't in his inner circle you couldn't get close enough to try. Don't get me wrong, though. Koenig is charismatic, and those who follow him do so blindly and with great passion . . . like my nephew Heinrich."

"Heinrich?" Colt asked. The hair on the back of Colt's neck was standing on end.

"You know him?" Sheriff Sutherland asked.

Colt nodded. "He was crushed in a cave-in in the tunnels under the CHAOS Military Academy."

"That doesn't surprise me," Sheriff Sutherland said, his voice devoid of emotion. "He was a good kid, but when his mother died, Koenig was there to infuse his brand of hatred and revenge, and my nephew bought into it."

"Does Koenig fear the Betrayer?"

"He fancies himself a god," Sheriff Sutherland said. "I'm not sure he fears anything."

"What about you? Do you think the prophecy is real?"

"I can only hope." The sheriff coughed, and his breathing grew ragged. "If the salvation of humans and Thule alike comes through a person called the Betrayer, it will be because God wills it. And that's the truth I hold on to."

A blast shook the holding cell, and a child screamed for her mother. Her voice was swallowed by a cacophony of bombs and bullets as the holding cell echoed with the sound of metal grinding against metal.

The room dipped to the left. And then they fell.

Metal crunched, and Colt could hear the echo of gunshots from somewhere beyond the walls. People scrambled to sit upright, groaning and choking as they strained against their collars. Colt fought to break free from his bonds, desperate to help the people around him.

There was a sound like keys rattling, and a door fell open like the door of an oven. A silhouette, black against the amber light, ducked through. Something stood in the middle of the prisoners with a pistol in each of its six hands.

More shouting. Gunshots. Fighting. Bodies fell, and someone else stepped through the doorway. Colt's line of sight was obscured by the Thule, but whoever it was, he didn't have six arms.

The Thule fired one of the pistols and was about to fire another when a bolt of blue electricity shot across the room, hitting it in the chest. The electricity crackled across its body as it fell, leaving the stench of burning flesh.

Colt fought against the chains until he felt the trickle of warm blood flowing down each wrist. All around him were the sounds of moaning and whimpering. A woman sobbed as she stroked the hair of a little girl who didn't move. An old man lay against the wall, his neck bent at an odd angle, his mouth slightly open and his eyes staring straight ahead.

There was movement near the doorway as a dozen men entered the room, weapons at the ready. One walked to the fallen Thule and kicked it with his boot. Colt couldn't see his face, but it sounded like he was speaking Thule.

Colt strained to break free. Tendons popped out of his neck, and as metal tore into his flesh, the trickle of blood turned to a steady flow. He pressed harder. The cut ran deeper. The man stood there watching him like a father might watch his son throw a temper tantrum.

"It's not worth it," the man said, this time in perfect English. "The best you'll do is tear your hands off at the wrist. Then there's the bacteria, not to mention the smell of your blood, which will no doubt draw the Riek. This is their hunting ground, and nightfall will be here soon."

He stepped into the light, and Colt recognized the eye patch and the scar that ran down his face and across his lip. "Agent Rhane?"

"That's Commander Rhane, Soldier of the Grail."

CHAPTER 43

C olt froze, uncertain if he should be frightened or relieved. Soldiers of the Grail were supposed to be sworn enemies of Koenig's Defense Corps. And there was the fact that Rhane had helped Colt train for Project Betrayal back on campus . . . but did Agent O'Keefe and the others know that he was one of *them*—that he was a Thule? *They had to know*, Colt told himself. *Right?*

"Look, you've got more questions than I have time to answer," Rhane said, as though he had been reading Colt's thoughts. "The way I see it, you have two choices. You can come with us or you can stay here and face Koenig's Defense Corps when they come looking for you—that is, if the Riek don't get hold of you first."

Rhane stood there, expressionless, his good eye lingering on Colt. Probing. Searching. Then, without a word, he turned and walked over to the fallen Thule and fished a set of keys from a pouch that hung from its belt. He unlocked Colt's bonds and led him out of the transport and into a jungle that looked like one of the training scenarios from the hologram room—but this time it was real.

Trees draped in vines rose high overhead, their canopy of leaves blotting out the sun. The temperature was overwhelming and the air was thick, making it hard to breathe. Much of the ground was covered in standing pools that were dotted with cattails and lily pads, and Colt watched as winged frogs, bright yellow with red spots, flew over the water's surface.

From what he could see there were at least thirty Soldiers of the Grail, some in their native Thule form while others looked human. They scampered along the fallen transport, scavenging parts and loading them into a cart pulled by a creature the size of an elephant, though with its massive hump, round head, and tusks jutting out from its wide jaw, it looked more like a mutated rhino.

Colt squinted and wiped the moisture from his brow, wondering what to do. Project Betrayal wasn't supposed to take place for another ten days, and he was supposed to have the rest of Phantom Squad at his side, not to mention support from Jackal, Blizzard, Lightning, and Anvil. Instead, here he was on Gathmara with a renegade army of Thule, and he was fairly certain that the only thing keeping them from splitting him open and eating his liver was the fact that they thought Colt was somehow going to help them destroy Aldrich Koenig and his Defense Corps.

"I wasn't kidding about the infection," Rhane said as he snapped off a meaty leaf from what looked like an oversized aloe plant. He ran his thumbnail down the center, squeezed out a clear gelatinous liquid that smelled like lemon, and rubbed it on Colt's wrists. "It's called evros, and it does wonders for surface wounds."

"Thanks," Colt said. It was cold and at first it stung, but it didn't take long before soothing relief set in. As he stood there he caught sight of armed soldiers escorting the other prisoners to an armored vehicle with eight oversized tires. It looked a bit like a Stryker, but it was built for cargo, not warfare.

There were at least two dozen prisoners, and each of them silently clambered into the back with their heads down and shoulders slumped. The only one Colt was able to make eye contact with was Sheriff Sutherland, but one of Rhane's soldiers pushed the sheriff into the back of the vehicle before he could speak.

Colt frowned and took a step forward, but Rhane grabbed him by the arm. "They're not your concern," he said. "At least not for now."

"What are you going to do with them?"

Before Rhane could answer, a roar like an engine spooked a flock of birds, and they took to the sky. Moments later something that looked like a cross between a helicopter and a fighter jet was looming overhead.

"What is that thing?" Colt asked.

"One of Koenig's hovercraft," Rhane said. "We took their prize and they want it back."

"Their prize?"

"You." Rhane turned to the other soldiers. "We're heading out. Now!"

"Wait," Colt said. "You knew I was in that transport?"

Rhane didn't reply as he led Colt into the trees to where an armored Walker with six mechanical legs instead of four normal tires was parked. There was a flurry of activity as the Soldiers of the Grail gathered their gear and loaded the other vehicles.

A band of Twilek swung from branch to branch, their screams echoing through the jungle as the ground transport with all the prisoners in the back rumbled to life. There was a sound like metal grating on metal as the driver put it into gear. Exhaust spilled from dual smokestacks as the vehicle moved down a path that looked far too narrow.

Trees shook as Koenig's hovercraft drew near. It was close enough that when Colt looked up through the branches he could see the insignia of the Defense Corps on the underbelly. Guns mounted on the hovercraft started to fire, and flares of orange erupted from the barrels. Colt turned and covered his head as bullets tore through the vegetation.

"Let's go!" Rhane shouted as he jumped into the driver's seat of the armored Walker.

Shrapnel bounced off the Walker as Colt slid underneath, scrambling to get to the passenger's door. There was shouting. Someone screamed, and Colt watched as a Soldier of the Grail fell nearby, his lifeless eyes open and his mouth agape.

"Now!"

Rhane's voice shocked Colt into motion and he rolled out from under the vehicle, opened the door, and climbed into the passenger's seat. The Walker jolted forward, pounding through pools of dead water and skittering over moss-covered boulders as the hovercraft tracked them through the branches overhead.

Soon the ground started to shake, and moments later a herd

of what looked like six-legged elk thundered across the path up ahead. Each was as big as a draft horse, with a long tail that ended in a set of wicked spikes. Their eyes looked crazed as they fled before the hovercraft overhead.

Rhane broke hard to the left and into a wide clearing. There was a roar like an engine, and the hovercraft dropped down with its nose pointed at the Walker. A spray of bullets erupted from the guns lodged under the wings, ricocheting off the armor. The windshield splintered but didn't break as Rhane reached over and flipped open a panel. "See those red switches? Flip 'em on."

Colt did as he was told, and panels opened up on either side of the hood, revealing a set of machine guns. They opened fire, tearing through the leaves and branches. Bullets sprayed the hovercraft, pounding against metal and glass.

"Looks like we're going to need some extra firepower," Rhane said. "See the RPG-7 in the back?"

Colt looked over his shoulder to see a rocket-propelled grenade launcher resting on the floorboards.

"It's loaded with a Thermobaric warhead," Rhane said. "Think you can handle it?"

"How hard can it be?" Colt unstrapped his seat belt, grabbed the grenade launcher, and leaned out the window, bracing his hip against the door.

The Walker dipped as they went through another pool, and Colt barely managed to keep from falling out. The hovercraft held its ground and bullets continued to fly, but Colt tried to ignore them as he took aim.

The hovercraft was in his sights. *Just aim, exhale, and pull the trigger,* Colt told himself. The warhead hissed as it left the launcher. Colt watched it streak through the air before it slammed into the hovercraft. There was a flash of light followed by an explosion, and the hovercraft spiraled out of control and slammed into the ground.

:: CHAPTER 44 ::

I just got word that there's another transport," Rhane said, pointing to his comlink as they continued through the jungle in the strange Walker. "They think it has more prisoners from Earth."

"Where is it?" Colt asked as he looked at the GPS hologram map that floated over the dashboard.

"About three clicks from here, and Koenig has already sent a Tracker to make sure there aren't any surprises. But if we hurry we should have enough time to get in and out before it finds us."

Colt noticed another Walker skittering through the jungle beside them, and then he saw two more, plus five or six armored ultralights and a massive machine that looked like a tank on eight mechanical stilts. It resembled the Walkers but was twice as big, with heavy armor casing and topped with a gun turret.

"This seems like as good a spot as any for an ambush," Rhane said. He parked beneath the cover of something that looked like a red mushroom, though it was nearly as big as a garage. The other vehicles stopped as well, each one with its weapons systems pointed toward the sky.

Colt felt anxious as he sat there, wondering if any of the prisoners inside the Thule transport might be his friends or maybe Jonas's mom or even the sheriff of Sanctuary. And he wondered how they were going to knock the transport out of the sky without killing everyone inside.

"Steady now," Rhane said as the air started to buzz with the sound of an engine in flight. "I can see her in the distance."

Eyes narrowed, Colt looked at the sky and saw the faintest speck of gray approaching. He watched as Rhane again flipped open the panel that controlled the weapons systems.

"Just a few more seconds," Rhane said. "Hang on, we're—"

The ground started to shake and the trees swayed back and forth. There was a cracking sound like wood splitting, and Colt turned to see a massive Tracker heading directly toward them.

"Now there's a twist I didn't expect," Rhane said. He accelerated and headed directly for the Tracker, guns blazing as the bullets ricocheted off the giant mechanical monster. The Tracker's chest opened like a set of elevator doors, revealing a bank of sixteen missiles that all fired at once. Spinning and swirling, they headed straight for Rhane's Walker.

There was an explosion as something like a lightning bolt shot out from the massive tank-like contraption with the gun turret. The Tracker's missiles died as they came in contact with the energy field, and the bolt struck the Tracker in the chest.

Energy crackled along its surface, and a second later the lights behind its eyes went out.

"What was that?" Colt asked.

"Think of it as an electromagnetic pulse with a kick."

The Tracker teetered and fell, but there was no time to celebrate. The gun turret took aim at the transport in the sky and unleashed a second blast of energy.

"Nice shot," Rhane said as he watched it hit. Bolts like lightning danced across the bulk of the transport. The engines sputtered before they failed, and smoke trailed as it started to fall.

"Let's go find us some prisoners," Rhane said, taking off at a trajectory that led them toward the path of the falling vehicle. Its hull struck the top of the trees and then crumpled when it struck a trunk. There was a crash of splintering wood and snapping trees, followed by an explosion.

Rhane and Colt were first on the scene, and they watched as the engine spit flames of red, orange, and gold as smoke rose through the canopy of trees. There were sounds like people pounding against the wall, and Rhane didn't hesitate. He grabbed a blowtorch from the back of his vehicle and lit it midstride as he raced toward the wreckage.

The other Soldiers of the Grail weren't far behind, and they joined Rhane as he cut open a doorway in the metal husk of the transport. His soldiers entered with weapons raised, but they didn't need them. There was no resistance from Koenig's men as the prisoners from Earth were led out.

Colt didn't recognize anyone at first and was giving up hope when he saw Oz, followed by Danielle and Pierce, who had a massive gash on his forehead.

"That's my squad!" he cried, just as Oz said, "Look! There he is."

Before Colt could reach them, a pair of Soldiers of the Grail stepped in front of him with guns drawn.

"Where do you think you're going?" the first one asked.

"They're with me," Colt said. "They're part of the mission."

||||||||||||||||||||||||||||||

Rhane led them all through the remains of what had once been a city.

Pierce was walking with a noticeable limp. Though he insisted that he was fine, Colt was fairly certain that his squadmate's ankle was broken and found a walking stick to help support his weight.

They could just make out the rough shapes of buildings beneath the creeping vines. Some were sagging and others had fallen over. Trees grew out of windows and pools of stagnant water covered the streets, creating the perfect breeding ground for insects.

"I don't understand why tourists don't like this place," Oz said. "I mean, look at that." He pointed at a spider that was the size of a bicycle tire. It was black and hairy with bright yellow stripes and was clinging to a web as thick as a rope.

"That's disgusting," Danielle said.

"Vrolek spiders are a delicacy," Rhane said. "They taste a bit like chicken, though the consistency is more like porridge."

Danielle crinkled her nose. "Double disgusting."

"How much farther?" Pierce asked. The cut on his head had stopped bleeding but it looked infected, and sweat was beading on his forehead.

"We're here." Rhane pulled back a curtain of vines and revealed a metal staircase that led up to the second floor of a crumbling building. Strange phosphorescent fungus clung to the exterior walls, and water trailed down the surface like tears.

"What is this place?" Colt asked.

"Nowhere important," Rhane said as two of his men stood guard at the base of the stairs. He led the remnant of Phantom Squad through a door and down a hall until he came to an empty apartment. Other than a table and some broken chairs, there wasn't much in the way of furniture, and the only light source was a series of windows buried under thick vines.

"Then what are we doing here?" Pierce asked, his voice weak, though his words were sharp. He glared at Rhane even as he leaned against the wall, chest heaving. Each labored breath produced a sound like rattling bones. Before anyone could react, his eyes rolled up in the back of his head and he fell over.

"Pierce!" Danielle rushed over and placed her head against his chest. "I don't think he's breathing."

"He's infected," Rhane said.

"Can't you do something?" Danielle asked.

"Possibly," Rhane said. "But I'm not making any promises."

Danielle stroked Pierce's forehead while Colt and Oz, at Rhane's command, went in search of the driest wood they could find. When they got back, Rhane started a small fire right next to the window and soon had a small pot of water boiling on the open flame. He pulled out a pouch and added what looked like dried herbs and tea leaves. The concoction smelled like a wet towel that had been sitting in the bottom of a gym bag for the better part of a semester.

"I need one of your socks," Rhane said.

"Don't look at me," Danielle said. "I'm not taking my boots off with those spider things running around."

"Fine, I'll do it," Colt said. He removed one of his boots and then his sock and handed it to Rhane, who proceeded to scoop the leaves out from the pan and place them inside the sock. When he was finished he placed it on Pierce's wound.

"Now what?" Danielle asked.

Rhane shrugged. "If he's still breathing in the morning, then I give him a better than average shot at surviving."

"But—"

"He'll make it," Colt said.

Danielle wiped a tear from her eye. "I hope so."

"I don't mean to sound like a jerk," Oz said, "but we have bigger issues at the moment."

"He's right," Rhane added. "Koenig knows that Colt is here, which means he's going to accelerate his plan to invade Earth."

"I thought he didn't believe in the prophecy," Danielle said.

"That's what he likes to tell people," Rhane replied. "But he isn't willing to take any chances. Besides, he needs to attack before his treaties with the Dagon Alliance and the Vril fall apart, just like his treaty with the Black Sun Militia. That was a devastating blow."

"How long do we have?" Colt asked.

"From everything we can tell, less than twenty-four hours." Rhane pulled out a metal disc the size of a coaster. He pressed a button, and a holomap of Dresh appeared.

"Why are you doing this?" Colt asked. "I mean, if this world dies, you're going to die with it, so why are you helping us? Why not invade Earth so you can survive?"

"Because if Koenig succeeds it will only be a matter of time before he destroys your planet, just as he destroyed ours," Rhane said. "Besides, we don't believe all hope is lost here on Gathmara. But before we can heal our land, we have to get rid of the man who poisoned it."

He walked over to a closet and pulled out a black duffel bag, which he unzipped and placed in the center of the floor. "It's not quite what you're used to, but it should do."

Inside the duffel were explosives and detonators, along with goggles, a pair of boots, and guns. There were even magnetic grenades, grappling hooks, pulse charges, and clips for the sidearms.

"Grab what you can carry and then try to get some sleep," Rhane said. "We head out in five hours."

"This is it?" Colt said as he pulled out a Luger that looked like it had been used during the Second World War. "What about body armor?"

"Afraid that I'm fresh out," Rhane said. "After all, we Thule don't exactly need armor, now do we?"

:: CHAPTER 45 ::

It was still dark when Colt woke up the next morning to the sound of hushed voices.

He cracked open an eyelid and saw Oz snoring while a red lizard with a bright blue underbelly crawled over his friend's hand, up his arm, and then up the wall and out the window. Danielle was curled up beneath a thin blanket next to the remnants of the fire, and Rhane was on the other side of the room kneeling next to Pierce.

"Yeah, I'm fine," Pierce was saying as he sat with his back against the wall.

"It's better that you stay here and—"

"Why are you in such a rush to get rid of me?"

Rhane shook his head. "Then at least drink this," he said, handing Pierce a mug with steam coming off it.

Pierce brought it to his nose and sniffed. "What is it?"

"Our version of an energy drink," Rhane said.

"No thanks." Pierce set the mug to the side and tried to stand, but he collapsed back to the floor, his face contorted.

"That one is going to get us all killed," Rhane said as he walked over to where Colt lay. "His ankle is broken and he still has a fever."

"I'll talk to him," Colt said. The first vestiges of sunlight shone through the window, and as Colt stood he could just make out Dresh in the distance. Countless buildings created an uneven landscape, and smokestacks belched endless plumes that rose to join vast clouds the color of steel wool.

They ate a quick breakfast as they listened to Rhane's plan. Pierce relented and drank Rhane's concoction, and within minutes he was strong enough to pack his gear and head downstairs with the others.

"You're sure that you're okay?" Colt said.

"Never felt better," Pierce replied as he shouldered an assault rifle, but Colt could tell by the weakness in his voice, not to mention his chalky complexion, that he was lying.

Rhane drove Pierce in the Walker while Colt, Danielle, and Oz followed on armored ultralights. Though it was early, the temperature was already sweltering. The aviator goggles that Colt wore kept steaming over, and he had to stop more than once to clean them off.

The Twilek were already out, plucking insects from their fur and feeding on bright red fruit with green flesh. The juice ran down their lips and onto their coats, but they didn't seem to mind. A flock of Ryax took to the sky as the vehicles rushed past their nesting area, and Colt thought he caught a glimpse of a Riek before it disappeared into the shadows.

They parked half a click outside Dresh in the middle of a

swamp teeming with wildlife. Rhane led them the rest of the way by foot, fighting through the thick vegetation and steamy air. Half an hour later they had reached the outskirts of Dresh, but they stopped when Rhane raised his hand.

"What's wrong?" Colt asked, his voice barely a whisper.

Rhane nodded toward the distance. "Soldiers from the Dagon Alliance," he said. "You can tell by their markings. See those squid-looking things on their arms?"

"We're going to take them out, right?" Oz said, sliding the strap of his assault rifle off his shoulder so he could hold it at the ready.

"No," Rhane said. "We can't afford the distraction."

"I can hit a fly on top of a soda can from a hundred yards away," Oz said.

"It has nothing to do with your marksmanship," Rhane said. "We don't want to lose track of our primary mission, and we definitely don't want them sounding the alarm and alerting their friends. Besides, I can guarantee you that there are hovercraft scanning the jungle, not to mention the Trackers that our scouts spotted earlier this morning."

Oz shouldered his assault rifle with obvious reluctance, eyeing the soldiers of the Dagon Alliance until there was too much vegetation and too many shadows between them.

Soon they stepped foot on the first crumbling street of Dresh. All around them flowering vines choked the dilapidated buildings. A lizard the length of a broomstick jumped from its perch with arms and legs spread, relying on parachute-like membranes that attached from its front to back ankles as it glided from building to building.

"Where is everybody?" Danielle asked as they walked down an empty street.

"Most citizens have fled to the jungle," Rhane said. "Those who remain stay locked inside their homes, fearful to come out and face the wrath of Koenig's Defense Corps."

No sooner had the words left Rhane's lips than Colt spotted two figures at the other end of the street, heading toward them. One was a Thule in its native reptilian form with a red armband; the other looked human and was dressed in a crisp gray military uniform.

"This way," Rhane said as he ducked down an alley.

They heard the sound of marching feet, and soon hundreds of soldiers marched past, many carrying red banners with the symbol of the Defense Corps. Colt also noticed flags from the Dagon Alliance and the Vril, but there were no signs of the Black Sun Militia or the Soldiers of the Grail among the troops.

Just then Colt spotted movement in a window high overhead. Then he saw a spark, as if someone had lit a candle. The flame burned hotter and then arced out the window.

"Molotov cocktails!" Oz shouted as glass shattered on the pavement below. Fire erupted, and more bottles followed at once. The soldiers scattered. Some started shooting up at the windows while others took cover.

Two hovercraft lowered from the sky and opened fire at the empty windows. Cement and glass exploded. One of the hovercraft unleashed a series of sidewinder missiles that blasted a hole in the wall. A soldier fell, arms flailing and legs kicking. He changed from human to Thule in midair, but when he struck the ground he stopped moving.

"That's our cue," Rhane said, slipping out of their hiding spot and taking off down the street at a sprint.

Colt looked back at Pierce. "Can you keep up?"

"I'll be fine," Pierce said.

As Colt ran down the street, away from the fray, he caught sight of three animals that looked like a cross between a hyena and a wild pig, all feasting on some kind of roadkill.

"What are those things?" he asked as he ran alongside Rhane.

"Blurg," Rhane said.

The animals snorted and gulped, nipping at one another as they fought for scraps of food. Colt watched as one tore a hunk of flesh away and swallowed it whole, scales and all. His stomach churned and he tried to look away, but he couldn't.

Distracted, Colt didn't see the broken glass on the sidewalk. The sounds of shards crunching under his boots echoed across the too-empty street, and the animals turned to stare at him. Their long snouts were stained with blood, and their lips were curled back to reveal wicked teeth.

"Nice and easy," Rhane said. "All they want to know is that we aren't interested in their kill."

"Trust me, we're not."

⸻⸻⸻

"Over there." Rhane was crouched behind what looked like a trash bin. "See that barge?" He pointed down the street to a rusted boat scarred by scratches and dents. "That's the canal that will take us to the reactor station."

There was a sound like a turbine engine, and Colt looked

up between the buildings to see one of Koenig's hovercraft approaching.

"This way!" Rhane pulled him into what looked like an old butcher shop, and the other three members of Phantom Squad followed. Colt stood next to the front window and watched as the hovercraft descended until it was only ten feet off the ground. The roar of the turbines shook the walls as garbage spun through the air like it was caught in a tornado.

"Do you think they saw us?" Danielle asked.

"If they did, they'd be shooting," Rhane said.

Colt could feel his heart beating in his throat as he waited for the hovercraft to fly away. It seemed like hours even though it had only been a few minutes, but it finally left them alone.

"Let's go," Rhane said. "If they have search teams out, that means they think we're close. Everybody keep your eyes open."

Like Venice, Dresh was known for its intricate system of canals, but instead of gondolas there were rusted-out barges. The water was reddish-orange, and a disgusting froth clung to the surface along the cement walls that lined the canal.

"Not exactly the crystal blue waters of the Caribbean, is it?" Rhane said. Suddenly his face started to contort, and there was a sound like bone cracking. His skin bubbled and his muscles flexed, and a moment later he was standing there in his native Thule form.

At nearly eight feet tall, he looked a bit like a bearded dragon. He had massive shoulders and a powerful tail, and his body was covered in scales the color of honey. He had a short snout, and his back was lined with row after row of spikes. There were even clusters of spiny scales covering his throat.

Pierce took a step back, his index finger wrapped around the trigger of his assault rifle as he pointed the barrel at Rhane.

"If you think I'm ugly, wait until you run into Koenig," Rhane said as he wrapped his long toes around the edge of the canal. Nails like talons sank into the crumbling cement as he flexed them, his eyes now locked on the murky water.

"Is that sewage?" Danielle asked.

"Better you don't know," Rhane said, his tone flat.

"It doesn't matter, because it's our only way inside," Colt said as he removed his pack and took out his breathing apparatus.

"Just mind the Gorem and you'll be fine," Rhane said.

"Nobody said anything about Gorem," Oz said.

A chill ran down Colt's spine as he thought back to the enormous sea monster that had attacked Oz and him in the waterways beneath Trident Biotech. It had looked like a cross between an eel and an alligator, but it had three sets of arms and each one ended in a clawed hand.

"Are there really Gorem in there?" he asked.

It looked like Rhane smiled, though it was hard to tell with his reptilian face. "I guess we'll find out soon enough."

:: CHAPTER 46 ::

E'ven with fins it was difficult keeping up with Rhane, who used his tail to propel himself through the murky water like an alligator.

Visibility was practically nonexistent as they made their way through the underwater labyrinth. On more than one occasion Colt thought that he saw the silhouette of something enormous, but they managed to make it through the tunnel system without running into anything that could swallow them whole.

Rhane led them into a drainage system where a grate opened up into a storage room inside the facility. Once inside, Colt checked his backpack to make sure the detonators hadn't gotten wet while Rhane pulled up the holomap of the facility.

"Remember," Rhane said, "our singular goal is to get Colt inside that reactor room, and that means we do whatever it takes. Understood?" He was looking directly at Pierce, who started to cough.

"Yeah . . . I got it," Pierce said.

They were all surprised by how few guards patrolled the facility. Whenever a detail would approach, including the drones, they'd simply duck behind pipes or slip into empty stairwells until the Defense Corps soldiers passed. But Colt's heart nearly stopped beating when he almost ran smack into a Wächter.

Adolph Hitler's secret scientists first developed the Wächters—robots that had a narrow head atop broad shoulders and a wide breastplate, all painted red.

Colt stood there holding his breath as he waited for it to either shoot him or sound an alarm. But it didn't do either.

"Is it deactivated?" Danielle asked.

"I think so, but I'm not sure," Colt said. The light behind the robot's eye was dead, and Colt decided to tap its chest to see if it would respond.

"Let's go," Rhane said. "We don't have much time."

The robot's eye lit up. It raised its hand, releasing a stream of energy from a disc on its palm that knocked Rhane into the wall. Colt fumbled in his pouch for a magnetic grenade, but the Wächter was too quick. It knocked Colt's hand away and wrapped a claw around his arm.

"This wasn't part of the plan," Colt said, choking as an alarm sounded and red lights flashed across the ceiling.

Pierce raised his gun, but again the Wächter was too quick. A compartment opened on its forearm, revealing a Gatling gun. It opened fire, catching Pierce in the chest. He stood there, mouth agape as he watched plumes of red spread across his shirt. His eyes went to the Wächter and then to Colt, and blood started to pour from his lips.

Colt caught him as he fell.

"I'm sorry." Pierce coughed. "I . . . didn't . . ."

"It's okay," Colt said. "You're going to be fine."

"No . . . I'm not," Pierce said. "And . . . it's okay."

"Don't talk like that."

"Just . . . finish." Pierce closed his eyes. His breathing was rapid. "Finish it . . . and tell my dad . . ." Pierce went limp, and his head rolled back as his spirit left his body.

Colt felt the rage well inside of him and he leapt at the robot. Power surged as he tore its arm from its socket, using it as a club to beat its head until it caved in.

"That's enough," Oz said, but Colt kept pounding the Wächter. "Come on," Oz said. "We have to get out of here before more show up."

Colt stopped, chest heaving as he stood and looked at Pierce's motionless form.

"There'll be time to mourn when the battle is over," Rhane said. "Right now we need to finish what we started."

CHAPTER 47

Where are they?" Colt said as they followed Rhane through the empty hallways. "I mean, it's like this place was abandoned. There aren't even any drones."

He looked back at Danielle, whose eyes were filled with tears. She tried to force a smile but it didn't last long. Her hands were shaking and her breathing was shallow, like she was suffocating. Colt felt as though he was suffocating as well. He tried to push the image of Pierce lying there, dead, out of his mind, but he couldn't stop thinking about him.

"Koenig is probably marshaling his forces," Rhane said. "But he knows you're here to destroy the reactor, so leaving it unguarded doesn't make any sense."

"Unless it's a trap," Oz said.

"Even if it is, we don't have a choice," Colt said. He could feel the weight of the explosives resting in his backpack. "You got the portal cube ready?"

Danielle nodded.

"And you're sure you have the right coordinates?" Oz said. "The last thing I want to do is end up at the bottom of the ocean or the heart of a volcano."

"Not now," Danielle said.

"What? I'm serious," Oz said. "I was reading about it a couple nights ago when I couldn't sleep. All kinds of people died during the testing phase."

"The reactor room should be up around the—" Rhane stopped as he rounded the corner. There, standing at attention, were two rows of Koenig's Defense Corps, one on each side of the corridor. They were tall and muscular with long snouts, nostril slits, and glowing eyes of yellow that shone bright against their onyx scales.

"How many?" Oz asked, removing his assault rifle.

"Too many for us to handle," Rhane said.

Has the Betrayer come to realize his destiny? Colt couldn't see Koenig, but his words were invading Colt's mind.

Come then, don't be shy. And please, bring your friends to bear witness. After all, it's not every day that you get to watch the extinction of an entire race.

Colt concentrated, trying to form the words in his mind. *What about your Defense Corps?*

They won't harm you, Koenig said. *You have my word.*

"What's going on?" Oz said when he noticed the look on Colt's face.

"It's Koenig," Colt said. "He wants us to go into the reactor room."

"It's definitely a trap," Oz said.

"Maybe. We're about to find out." Colt grabbed the medallion that his grandpa had given him and started to walk down the hall toward the reactor. "And remember, whatever happens, God is our refuge and strength, a very present help in trouble."

Colt tensed as he walked past the first of Koenig's Defense Corps members. The aliens were enormous, standing at least eight feet tall, with broad shoulders, wicked teeth, and curved horns. Hands sweaty and mouth dry, Colt willed himself to take one step and then another until he made it to the doors.

"What, you didn't think we'd follow you?" Oz said when he caught Colt turning around. "Brothers to the end, remember?"

"Brothers to the end," Colt said.

The doors opened, and inside the reactor room was a vast circular space with concrete walls and a wide ledge all around. In the center of it all was a deep chasm. Light pulsed from the depths, casting the entire room in blue—including Aldrich Koenig, who was standing on the ledge in human form.

I have to admit, Koenig said, *I'm thoroughly impressed. I never thought you'd make it this far.*

Colt looked past Koenig to the chasm. All he had to do was set the charges and toss the backpack into the reactor core while Danielle opened up the portal that would take them back to Sanctuary.

Yes, there it is, Koenig said. *You're so close to fulfilling your destiny, and yet . . .* He paused as his Defense Corps marched into the room and stood at attention against the wall like they were some kind of living statuary.

Colt slipped the backpack off his shoulder.

I'm afraid I can't let you do that. Koenig's face contorted and skin bubbled as he morphed into his native Thule form. His clothes ripped away and without pause he charged at Colt.

Rhane stepped between them, teeth bared and claws outstretched. He lashed out, and Koenig batted his arm to the side. Rhane tried again and then again, but each time Koenig caught his blows. With a quick flick of his wrist, Koenig tossed Rhane aside.

"This is between myself and the Betrayer," Koenig said as once more his clawed fingers lashed out.

Colt felt a searing pain, and blood trickled down his cheek. Koenig lashed out again, this time raking his claws across Colt's chest. Colt tried to counter, but even with his enhanced speed and strength from the Thule DNA, he was too slow, his body too weak. Koenig easily fended off his strikes.

Koenig grabbed Colt by the arm with one hand and ripped the backpack away from his shoulders with another. He tossed it aside. His tail swishing back and forth, Koenig walked over to the chasm and dangled Colt over the ledge. "It's time for you to die."

He let go, and as Colt fell he managed to grab hold of the ledge. His fingers ached as his feet scrambled to find footing. For a brief moment he glanced down and started to panic when he couldn't see the bottom. *Don't look,* he told himself. With a surge of strength, he reached out and took hold of Koenig's ankle.

"God is our refuge and strength, a very present help in trouble," Colt said aloud as he pulled with all his might.

Koenig teetered, and as he fell, Colt pulled himself up onto the ledge. Koenig screamed, his six arms flailing to grab hold of something. Anything.

Colt's eyes never left the Defense Corps soldiers as they stood there looking confused. Whatever their plan had been, watching their leader plummet to his death most certainly was not a part of it. Colt scrambled to the backpack. He unzipped it and set the detonator, willing his fingers to work.

"Get that portal cube ready!" he said.

The moment the detonator was set, the Thule soldiers sprang to life. Teeth gnashed and tails pounded as they ran for Colt, but it was too late. He took his backpack and threw it over the chasm, while at the same time Danielle hit the Enter button on the portal cube.

"What are you waiting for?" Colt felt the claws of a Thule rake across his back as he watched Danielle jump through the portal. The Thule raised its hand to strike again, but Colt ducked and caught it in the nerve cluster just below its jaw.

Oz went through the portal next, but when Colt turned he saw Rhane getting attacked by one of Koenig's soldiers. "Go!" Rhane shouted. "I'll be right behind you."

Colt hesitated, then turned and ran just as the first of the explosions erupted. There was another and another. The ceiling cracked overhead and massive chunks of cement fell, shattering as they hit the ground.

"Come on!" Colt shouted.

He jumped toward the portal, and as he turned one last time he watched Rhane break free and try to follow, only to be overwhelmed by the Defense Corps soldiers. There was another explosion, followed by a flash of light. Colt was thrown through the air, and the last thing he remembered before he blacked out was that he hit something hard.

:: CHAPTER 48 ::

It was over.

At least that's what the president said during his State of the Union address. Koenig was dead and the Defense Corps all but destroyed, but that didn't mean it was over—not completely, anyway. Still, the Intergalactic Defense Academy decided to give their cadets a monthlong sabbatical, and Grandpa decided to treat the surviving members of Phantom Squad to a week on the beach in San Diego.

Colt sat on his surfboard a hundred yards from shore while Lily sat next to him, the water calm as the sun rose behind them. He desperately wanted to enjoy the moment. He should have been happy. He had not only accomplished the mission, but he was back home with the girl of his dreams. And yet in the stillness of the morning his thoughts continued to drift to his parents. Captain Starling. Pierce. So many losses. So much heartache.

"What are you thinking about?" Lily asked.

Colt smiled. "Did you know that the last time I was out here I got attacked by a sea monster?"

"Are you trying to freak me out?"

"I thought it was seaweed or something, but before I knew what was happening a tentacle wrapped around my ankle and pulled me under. But don't worry. I won't let it get you." He looked over at Lily as she sat on her surfboard in a black wet suit with hot pink sleeves. She was beautiful, even without makeup. Her lips were full, her blue eyes even bluer against the water, and her long blond hair, wet from the sea spray, was swept back over her head.

"Sorry," he said. "It's just that it seems like a lifetime ago."

"It was," Lily said. "You were a different person then. So was I. But we've changed. The world has changed."

"No kidding." Colt looked toward the shore, where Glyph and Jonas were building a sand sculpture. It was eight in the morning on a weekday, but they were already drawing a crowd of onlookers as they crafted an incredibly lifelike dragon that looked like it was going to be the size of a fishing boat by the time they finished.

"I really like your friends," she said, reaching out to take Colt's hand.

"Yeah. They're great."

"And I'm sorry about what happened to Pierce."

"Thanks," Colt said.

"So now what?" Lily said. "I mean, you saved the world. Where do you go from here?"

"I don't know," Colt said. "The DAA still wants to put together a touring Phantom Flyer show."

"Are you going to do it?"

"I'm not sure," Colt said. "I mean, to be honest all I want to do right now is sleep, but I kind of feel like I owe it to Captain Starling. After all, it was his idea."

"He was the flight instructor?"

"Yeah." Colt closed his eyes as an image of Captain Starling dead in the tunnels flashed in his mind. "His nephews are Phantom Flyer fans, and I was thinking that since he didn't have any kids of his own, I could try and get them a part in the show."

"I always knew you were one of the good guys."

"I guess." Colt watched a pelican soar overhead. "You know, they're talking about having musical acts too. I guess they reached out to Switchfoot and Casting Crowns."

"Are you serious?"

"I told them the only way I'd do it is if you get to be in the act."

"Don't mess with me, Colt McAlister."

"If you want it, you're in."

A wide smile broke across her face as she lunged and wrapped her arms around him. The momentum sent them both tumbling into the water. They laughed as they embraced, and the warmth of her lips against his cheek sent a tingling sensation down his spine.

"What about Oz and Danielle?" she asked, wrapping her arm around her surfboard.

Colt did the same. "Have you heard them sing?"

"That's not what I meant."

"Danielle would run the special effects, and Oz would be one of the Agents of CHAOS. Same goes for the rest of Phantom

Squad." Colt smiled. "Grandpa even agreed to tour with us. He said he won't fly, but I have a feeling he might."

"But what happens after that?" she asked. "I mean, the tour won't last forever. Do you think they're going to make you go back to the academy, or will you be able to go to college?"

"Grandpa says the president still wants me to become the Phantom Flyer full-time, but to tell you the truth, I don't know if I'm cut out to be a superhero."

"If anybody is, you are." She poked the end of his nose with her finger, and he reached over and brushed the hair from her eyes.

"We're not interrupting anything, are we?"

Colt turned to see Oz and Danielle paddling toward them on their surfboards.

"Not really," Lily said. "We were just talking about the future."

"So were we," Oz said as Danielle rolled her eyes. "You know, you're going to need an agent, McAlister. Someone to manage your endorsements and make sure you're getting the big bucks for your appearance fees."

"Let me guess," Colt said. "You?"

"Why not?" Oz said. "I was thinking, the first thing we should do is make a video game."

"Ridiculous, right?" Danielle said.

Colt shrugged. "I don't know. I kinda like it."

It was faint at first, but Colt could hear the sound of an engine. He looked up to see an XSR Interceptor speeding toward them.

"Friends of yours?" Oz asked.

"I don't think so," Colt said.

Oz looked over his shoulder. "There's no way we can make it back to shore before they catch us."

"Then we might as well find out what they want." Colt pulled himself up on his surfboard and sat there waiting for the patrol vessel to approach. It was steel gray, and as it neared, the only marking Colt could see was an insignia that looked like a Thule skull and crossbones.

It didn't take long before it pulled up next to them. There were two men on board, both wearing dark suits, tinted sunglasses, and white earpieces.

"My name is Agent Johnson," the larger of the two said. "This is Agent McAndrew. We're with the Department of Alien Affairs."

"Yeah, we kind of figured that, what with the logo and everything," Oz said.

Agent Johnson ignored him. "Director Montgomery expresses his deepest regret, as we understand you just arrived in San Diego last night, but I'm afraid we have need of your services."

"What services?" Colt asked.

"We believe that a geneticist in Argentina is breeding Dog Men," said Agent Johnson.

"No way," Oz said, breaking into a wide smile.

"That's supposed to be bad news, right?" Danielle said.

"Yes, ma'am," Agent Johnson said.

"You'll have to forgive him," she said, patting Oz on the shoulder. "He's not exactly the sharpest tool in the shed."

"Let me guess," Colt said. "The DAA wants us to hunt them down?"

"Yes, that's correct."

"We're in!" Oz said.

All eyes turned to Colt, who was staring at the water.

"Cadet McAlister?" Agent Johnson said.

Colt turned to the agent and smiled. "Yeah, we're in."

CHAOS SKETCHES

Lohr

Phantom Flyer

Lt. McAlister

Thule Warrior

D3.X

Images from Invasion
by Kyle Latino

Lobo Romero
by Enrique Rivera

Oz Romero
by Enrique Rivera

Danielle Salazar
by Danny Araya

Thule
by Danny Araya

Images from Alienation

Colt McAlister by Phil Hester

Colt McAlister by Evan Shaner

Colt McAlister by George Sellas

READING GROUP GUIDE

1. With Oz expelled from the CHAOS Military Academy, Colt feels more alone than ever. Do you have a best friend? Have the two of you ever been separated for an extended period of time? How did that make you feel?

2. Colt volunteers to sequester himself because he's worried that he might hurt his friends. Have you ever had to sacrifice something that was important to you for the sake of someone else?

3. As Pierce taunts Jonas, dozens of cadets just stand there until Stacy and Colt intervene. Have you ever stood up to a bully on behalf of yourself or others?

4. Pierce acts like a jerk and yet Stacy defends him, insinuating that the pain in his life has caused him to act that way. Has anyone you've known experienced a depth of pain that could have changed their personality?

5. There's a time when Colt isn't sure about his feelings for Lily and Stacy, but in the end he picks Lily. Do you think it's possible for sixteen-year-olds to be in love? Why or why not?

6. Jonas has a secret that he's not willing to share with his new friends because he's afraid that they'll reject him if they know the truth.

7. Colt understood that there was a good chance that he wouldn't survive his last mission. What cause would you die for?

8. Colt thinks that creating a traveling air show starring the Phantom Flyer will only create false hope. Is false hope better than no hope at all?

9. The Thule are defeated, but it's only a matter of days before Colt is enlisted to fight another battle. Do you think that peace is attainable, or is life filled with one challenge after another?

ACKNOWLEDGMENTS

It's a rare thing to find someone who believes in you even when you lose faith in yourself . . .

Somewhere along the way I started listening to a distant voice that told me that I wasn't a very good writer. At first I was able to ignore it, but the seeds of doubt took root. I started believing lies, like I didn't belong. That I wasn't worthy. And that I didn't have a story worth telling.

I gave up on myself, but God brought people into my life who stood by me. I'd like to start by acknowledging them . . .

- Amanda Bostic, thank you for your patience and guidance. They have been a blessing in my life.
- Allen Arnold, you are a gentle shepherd and I appreciate all that you've done for me.
- Lee Hough, your prayers and your counsel helped bring calm in the storm.
- Kelly Lewis, you are a rock and the love of my life. Thank you for not giving up on me.

Thank you to my daughters, Bailey, Olivia, and Lauren, who fill my heart to overflowing every time I see your faces. Thank you to my parents, Brian Lewis and Annette Landgren, for the encouragement. Thank you to my in-laws (not a typo), Marlin and Shirley Broek, for the endless prayers. Thank you to the Crawford family for always believing in me. Thank you to Mike Reynolds for the same.

Thank you to Daisy Hutton and the entire Thomas Nelson Publishing team. It's an amazing organization from top to bottom. I appreciate your faith in this series.

Thank you to LB Norton, who is simply amazing in every sense of the word. You are a blast to work with!

Thank you to the amazing artists who contributed to the CHAOS series: Danny Araya, Mike Dubisch, Phil Hester, Reza ilyasa, Kyle Latino, Enrique Rivera, George Sellas, and Hoi Mon Tham.

Thank you to my Arizona friends who have been an amazing support system over the years . . . Faith "The Book Babe" Hochhalter, Brandi Stewart, Melanie Callahan, Michelle Aron, Daanon DeCock, Rebecca Paulson, Shannon and Bill Bailey, Jim Blasingame, Lisa Schell, Donna Powers, Lisa Bowen, Tim Loge, John and Sarah Morris, Joe and Freddie Boudrie, Bobbi Ackerman-Hedberg, Karen Knight, Barb Mackey, Denise Gary, Jean Beaird, Fran Bard, Mary Wong, Tuni Flancer, Jade Corn, and everyone at Changing Hands Bookstore and the Phoenix-area Barnes & Noble Booksellers.

Thank you to Tara Mylett and the amazing schools of Corpus Christi, Texas. Thank you to Traci Potter and Kitty Hawk Elementary School in Kitty Hawk, North Carolina. Thank you to Kelly Albaugh and Great Bridge Intermediate in Chesapeake, Virginia. Thank you to Mary Wollmering and Holy Spirit School in St. Paul, Minnesota. Thank you to Nancy Schwartz and all of the Johnston, Iowa, school district. Thank you to Lynne Reid and Alexander Dawson School in Las Vegas, Nevada. And thank you to all the other amazing schools and bookstores that have done so much to spread the word about this series. Thank you as well to everyone who has purchased one of the books I've written. You've truly helped make my dream of being an author come true.

And special thanks to Kathryn Mackel for all the work you put into making this story come to life. I couldn't have done it without you.

ABOUT THE AUTHOR

Photo by Scott Mitchell

Jon S. Lewis is the coauthor of the Grey Griffins trilogy and the Grey Griffins Clockwork Chronicles. He also writes for the DC COMICS family of publishers. He resides with his family in Arizona.